Wakefield Press

Gatherers and Hunters

Thomas Shapcott has published eleven novels, two previous collections of short stories and eighteen books of poetry. He has received many awards for his writing, including the Patrick White Prize and Senior Fellowships from the Australia Council, as well as an Order of Australia.

Professor Shapcott was the inaugural Professor of Creative Writing at the University of Adelaide (1997–2005). He has been Director of the Literature Board of Australia Council (1985–1990), Executive Director of the National Book Council (1992–1997) and a member of the Adelaide Festival Writers' Week Committee (2003–2006). In the period he was Professor of Creative Writing he wrote a number of the stories in *Gatherers and Hunters*. He now lives in Melbourne.

T0363974

Gatherers
and Hunters

stories by

Thomas Shapcott

**Wakefield
Press**

Wakefield Press
1 The Parade West
Kent Town
South Australia 5067
www.wakefieldpress.com.au

First published 2010

Cover design by Liz Nicholson, designBITE
Designed and typeset by Wakefield Press
Printed in Australia by Griffin Press, Adelaide

National Library of Australia Cataloguing-in-Publication entry

Author: Shapcott, Thomas W. (Thomas William), 1935–   .
Title: Gatherers and hunters/Thomas Shapcott.
ISBN: 978 1 86254 880 0 (pbk.).
Dewey Number: A821.3

Government
of South Australia

Arts SA

fox creek
wines

Australian Government

Publication of this book was assisted by
the Commonwealth Government through the
Australia Council, its arts funding and advisory body.

For Eva Hornung

Contents

Some of these stories have been initially published
in the following journals:

Alexandria (Belgrade)

Antipodes

Australian Short Stories

Griffith Review

Island

Imago

Refuge

Emre always rises at five. His palliasse has to be slid beneath the couch so that Frau Losberg might use the tiny room through the day for her piecework sewing. Emre is sincerely grateful for this space.

It is much more tolerable than the Migrant Hostel. His wife and daughter are still in the women's quarters but he is quite determined that must end. This present situation is only temporary, though he has been living in Frau Losberg's front room for ten weeks. An apartment – even if only two rooms – must be found somewhere. Adelaide, he has been told, and he believes it, has many houses split up into flats, sharing kitchen and bathroom space, but they are at least preferable to the dormitories and those inedible meals at the hostel.

As soon as he escaped the hostel, Emre was able to drag his precious typewriter from the leather suitcase, which was all he was able to bring with him. Its keyboard is Hungarian but he can manage English on it. Early on, he typed out on thick white paper many repetitions of his calling card and then cut them carefully to size: *Dr Emre Halasz Ll.D Translator and Linguist. Personal letters and documents. Typed and prepared to order.*

Frau Losberg's address was given. She had agreed to that on the promise of clear, typed copies of her tenancy agreements with all her lodgers, expressed as 'reimbursement of outlays and maintenance' to avoid Australian taxation watchdogs.

Emre's typing has always been meticulous, though he worries about the cost of a new typewriter ribbon. Every postage stamp has to be a consideration.

By 5.15 a.m. he is washed, shaved and dressed, his neat goatee scrupulously trimmed. No breakfast. The woollen suit still looks presentable; Frau Losberg turned the cuffs and collar excellently (in exchange for Emre painting the front exterior), assuring him there were years of use left in it if he does not wear out the pocket linings with objects. He pulls on his almost-new Homburg (a miracle from Anglicare) and affixes the bicycle clips. His first acquisition once he got out of the Migrant Hostel had been the attaché case. He keeps it oiled and polished, and made an attachment in front of the bicycle to carry it to work. The bicycle was a major investment, and he is still terrified that it will be stolen, or smashed, or a bomb will explode in the very street it is in – even though he has been assured, with rough but easy laughter by his workmates, that bombs do not go off in Adelaide. 'This isn't Europe, mate.'

Each time he rides it is a dare. He will be paying it off over the next two years. In his entire life he has never committed to anything this far in advance. The last seven years have been lived a day at a time, sometimes an hour at a time. Even when he and Marie had married, last year in Milano before embarkation, they had both thought of it as being not an insurance or a certain future but a vow to stick together for whatever time might be granted to them. The concept of a child had been almost unbearable – but real enough once the signs began to manifest. Marie had been more stoic than Emre. 'We shall see it through,' she said, knowing there was no alternative. By the time Kotie had been born – somewhere between Aden and Australia – they had both somehow come to the realisation that they were on a very long journey indeed and nothing they had been through might prepare them, either for parenthood or for the forthcoming tribulations.

Emre had been the first to consider plans. Marie had absorbed herself in the immense routine of feeding, bathing, comforting and accommodating the baby. Even the separation of the male and female quarters in the hostel did not seem to concern her much.

Emre had fretted right from the outset. Fatherhood may have taken him somewhat by surprise, but it also galvanised him in a way that was much more energising than the effort of their survival, which had been the only possible aim over these times. The voyage seemed endless, but out of it Emre had found time to think; and, through thinking, he had begun to plan.

To escape the grim prison-like regimentation and anonymity of the Migrant Hostel had been the first task. Achieved, the second had been to find some means of earning income.

Emre had been directed to an employment agency assisting migrants. He had filled in forms, in English, and listed his qualifications. The university degree and his years (1936 to 1943) as a newspaper journalist counted for nothing. Neither did his command of seven languages or his typing skills. He was allocated a shift-work labouring job in a vulcanising works from 6 a.m. to 4 p.m.

On his first day, fresh from the excitement of locating a corner in Frau Losberg's rooming house, and nervous over the audacity of committing himself to the bicycle with its fixed terms and outrageous interest payments, Emre had arrived ten minutes early, following the directions supplied by the employment agency on the back of an old printed circular on the Australian taxation 'deduction at source' system for employees. He had to stop under several streetlights to confirm road names and turns. He felt elated when he made it.

But his new workmates were another hurdle. They made noisy and disturbingly obscene comments on Emre's clothes – the suit, the white shirt and tie (borrowed), his leather gloves, the Homburg hat, and his attaché case. Sometimes it is a hindrance rather than a help to understand a language. Emre did not catch all the new words, nor the slippery, congested accents, but the general impression was absolute.

One older man with grizzled short hair and overalls directed him to the clerical section to fill in employment particulars and then to the change room, where Emre disrobed completely and picked out of his briefcase a fresh, laundered pair of overalls (he had been given previous instructions). His hands were soft and pale, true, but would harden up ('Piss on them,' his new foreman had said). In the refugee camps in Central Europe he had done his share of hard manual labour.

The vulcanising works was a place of extremes. Extreme heat. Extreme labour. Extreme language. Emre only had to ask a few times for directions to be repeated or explained. He was always willing, too willing. His workmates rebuked him, and he found it difficult to slacken his pace to meet the unspoken but definite requirement for minimum performance not maximum efficiency. In the lunch hours or at tea breaks, Emre was educated in the finer points of industrial restrictions. He kept his own counsel, and at the end of each shift, while the others slewed off to the pub and a few beers, Emre completely cleaned himself in the showers and dressed in his formal attire before affixing his clips and unlocking the gleaming bike from its safe place. He pulled on his gloves and set the Homburg at a firm angle before pushing off, back to the boarding house.

Only once had he been enticed to the pub with the other workers. That was after his first pay, and some of the group insisted he must shout them all a round. They had beers. Emre quietly asked for a white wine. He was chiacked ruthlessly; by the end of the first week he knew where he stood, and it was outside.

The gibes about his hat and his gloves and his 'bloody briefcase' had subsided. Within a month they would be proprietorial, proud of their resident 'Perfesser' on the vulcanising floor. But that first pay day, in the pub; Emre paid for his difference.

Eventually, though, he found he could remember several mildly salacious limericks from his university days (his English tutor preferred them to Keats and Shelley), and, to show his conviviality, he began quoting them. His accent broke them up. Before the session was over a couple of the younger ones had memorised his limericks and his accent.

Emre might have proved himself a 'good mate' but his pay packet was frighteningly depleted and he spent the bike ride home calculating where he must economise to make up. Breakfast was out. Now lunch must be eliminated also. Fortunately, he had discovered a Hungarian 'social club' where proper food could be obtained quite cheaply, if he did not indulge in the overpriced Barak Palinka.

His weekend 'business' as a translator and letter writer has been moving only in fits and starts. He had initially made contact with others in the Migrant Hostel, men who needed to fill out forms, or to write letters of supplication and appeal, or who could not even write. He supplied verbose and lying epistles to loved ones, or distant families, in Italy, in Austria, in Hungary.

But though Emre had busied himself in those early weeks of freedom with following up those contacts, and had even performed innumerable tasks of translation, or transcription, or letter writing, when it came to payment everybody was in the same boat. It was not going to earn him anything, except the burden of confidence over awkward confessions. Finally, he tore up the remaining business cards. The typewriter has been put back in storage.

His languages have failed him. For so long they had seemed almost a certain passport to small favours or to negotiable concessions. 'They can take everything but your education,' his mother had insisted. Here in Australia education seems to have been reduced to a fine sense of irony. 'What did you used to do?' one of his workmates asked him the other day. When he replied that he studied languages they crowed, almost as an ensemble: 'No, work. What work?' He had pretended not to understand, but that only brought ribald jokes. And it was true: the dialect they speak is often enough a different tongue to what he had studied even in Dickens and Somerset Maugham.

Frau Losberg has been insidious. Although she keeps offering suggestions for possible new accommodation and even allows Emre to peruse her Saturday *Advertiser* or *News*, the leads always turn out fruitless – rent too high, distance from his job too far, rooms too cramped or too squeezed for a family of three – and always when he returns, glum from another search, Frau Losberg almost inch by inch increases her attention. Emre finally has begun to understand.

In a sudden move he changes everything: he takes an apartment in the city. It consists of three upstairs rooms above a hairdresser's, and can only be reached through the shop itself. It is entirely illegal. And it has no kitchen and no water. Three bare rooms at the top of a creaking staircase. He has had to find a bed, and coverings, mattress, pillow, as well as things for the baby, and what about water?

With the help of a Czech plumber who owed him for a series of duplicitous letters to his wife, an Italian still waiting for him to send her the voyage money, they have managed to tap into a water main in the back lane and pass a copper pipe up the external wall (hidden by an overgrown creeper). At least there is, now, a tap. His plumber friend suggested a small spirits stove. There is no electricity upstairs either, he also discovers. Well, he could pick up a couple of kerosene lamps. Marie's cottage in the Austrian Tyrol had only such lighting.

When he feels he can do no more for the present he takes a bus to the Migrant Hostel. He returns with his family.

Frau Losberg was incensed when she heard, and threatened to tell the authorities. Emre only keeps her pacified by promising to paint the remaining external walls of her place. That means another month of weekends, which could have been more usefully employed, but it's worth it.

Marie looks at the apartment with its dusty green walls and bare boards and smiles at Emre shyly. From the window they stare out onto a brick wall across the alley.

'Look,' she says, and points to a small fern growing out of a crack in the bricks near the top. The baby keeps grizzling, she is teething. They spend their first night together for more than six months in the creaky bed with dusty blankets and only one pillow. The child seems to be restive between them and wakes almost every hour. She shits the bed. Emre has no sleep. He knows that he must rise at 4.30 in order to cycle the extra distance to the vulcanising works.

Between bouts of feeding and soothing the infant his wife sleeps solidly. Emre tries to remember when it was, how it was, that they first got together. Marie had fallen pregnant so quickly. For the first time he wonders: was that accidental?

Back then he had no thought of any coherent future. He only knew that his past had disappeared utterly. The apartment in Budapest had been long since taken over by the authorities and nationalised. His parents had not survived 1943. He knows only the blowsy woman who runs the 'Hungarian club' and two peasants from the voyage over who speak his language. Marie speaks German and has stubbornly refused to master English. Emre now tosses uncomfortably and tries not to rouse the stranger sharing his bed. A streetlight throws a yellowish rectangle upon the wall opposite. The prickly smell from the hairdresser's below cannot be ignored. For a brief moment he thinks of Frau Losberg's cosy, crowded front room. There are two oil paintings with huge frames: Alpine scenery, a secluded chalet. She has heavy drapes on the windows. It always reminds him of an aunt's apartment in Buda. He has no idea where his aunt is now, or what has become of her much-loved furnishings. Frau Losberg's little room has the musty warmth of memories. He knows he must never allow memories to crowd him. But for these moments he has seemed almost to be back there, though of course nothing can be the same.

The vulcanising works is his life now. Or for the foreseeable future. This is his existence, and it seems almost as tangible as razorwire fencing. Except that circumstances change. Even he has recognised that. One step at a time. One step then one step and even now he can look back and see the burden of despair and dulled endurance receding. The walls of this place, caught in that glare of light, carry echoes he will not remember. They will be simply one further item in the list of things he will not remember. But after his next pay he will take Marie to look for cheap curtain material. Unless she has other priorities. Which might well be so …

In all those years of servitude, flight, desperate and sudden displacements, transit camps, barracks, odd jobs and odder black market dealings, he has never thought of such simple but clearly articulated beginnings. Only endings. Each moment has been an end. Every new change is an end. His seven languages were all ends, interchangeable, isolating him internally while at the same time giving him a fluency others envied him for. He will cast off things here, as well as take things on. Language is a commodity, he has learned that. It is a tool of barter, not of emotions or feelings or human warmth. Warmth? There is only body warmth. Or body cold.

The first encounter with Marie: even that had seemed another ending, really leading nowhere, except for instant gratification. Instant sleep. Sleep.

It was the beginning.

Preparing to rouse himself, Emre thinks of the hot labour ahead and the rough and needy badinage of his workmates, and he realises his life has always been only beginning. It has taken him this long, and so many endings, to realise that he might, at last, be granted the luxury of looking forward. And that beginnings always lead onwards. Two years' time, he thinks. One year. The thought has him out of the bed (quietly, carefully, so as not to disturb the child. Or the mother), and the cold water for his shave pours out of the rickety tap like hopeful chatter.

The strange surroundings are already part of him, of his new present, and he realises that to remould this space will not be a task, it will be a discovery.

He laughs out loud so that the baby gives a startled cry and Marie reaches out her hand – not to Emre. Six months, he thinks. I will write this down, this room. No, I will get a camera and photograph it. In six months time we will look back and see how far we have come.

Has he even had such a thought before?

Carefully, he wheels the bicycle down the bumpy stairwell, careful not to scratch the walls. The cold air outside stings his eyes, but he wonders why he should be weeping.

The Red Hat

It wasn't that he feared his aunt, far from it. She moved swiftly and he had to keep up with her, no lagging. On the few times he stayed at her cottage overnight she was up so early it was indecent. That didn't bother his uncle, though. Nothing bothered Uncle Pat. Mark still remembered the first time, when he was woken – and to wake in a strange bed was a sort of dislocation anyway – and somewhere outside the thin window with its ancient brittle glass he heard a scratching sound. On and on.

Finally he could not bear the suspense. He raised his head and shoulders, glad for the thick flannelette pyjamas Aunt Olga had found for him (almost certainly a pair of Uncle Pat's), and then he peered out. His aunt was just below, weeding the garden bed along that side of the house – planting petunias, as it turned out. It must have been 5 a.m.

When he asked her at breakfast – boiled eggs and toast soldiers – why she had been up so early, she laughed and swiped her long, strong fingers through his tousled hair. 'I'll beat you up any day, boyo. Best time is early. Beat the sun to it, that's the idea. Want to join me tomorrow? There's that whole front bed needs planting.'

Only Aunt Olga could have dragged him out like that. Of course he was up and dressed and hovering on the little front verandah in time for her to sweep past like a rocket. She threw him a trenching tool (which he caught clumsily but without letting it clatter to the tiles) and was out and in action already. Uncle Pat always loafed in bed and waited for his morning cup at seven.

Aunt Olga was always there. So when his father remarked in passing, like that, without even a change in tone from the way he read the newspaper headlines like any other Tuesday morning, that Olga must be approaching the airport in KL at this minute, Mark was caught by surprise. 'Where is KL?' was his first question, but that was only a front, as it were. Nobody had told him.

When his mother explained that KL stood for Kuala Lumpur, in Malaysia, Mark already had dredged up that fact from his memory bank of TV travel features and that assignment he did; but the insult remained. 'How long is she going for? And Uncle Pat, did he go too?' He knew not to add, 'And why didn't they tell me?' He had been over there just two weeks before and had helped Aunt Olga harvest the last of the tomatoes, as well as bottling them. She had been in her most chatty mood. Now, he guessed why.

Uncle Pat was in Sydney for the week that Olga was off gallivanting, Mark's father explained, with one of those smiles to his mother that was beginning to get to Mark. He felt left out. There were codes and signals everywhere that were either new, or he had not noticed them before. His parents had included him in everything. As a kid he had been encouraged to speak up and 'dob in his pennyworth', as his dad used to say. Aunt Olga, in particular, listened and often as not dragged him into long arguments over something that really got him going, like Monkey or the game of Trivial Pursuit – in the days when Trivial Pursuit was a novelty of course. Before.

Before Grammar and before he overheard the reference to 'chatterbox' (though Aunt Olga had pounced on his dad for saying that; still, it had hurt). In the last year so many things had changed. It was crazy: the older he was growing, the more his parents treated him like a child; it was as if they could not see the changes in him.

It was as if he was neither the one thing nor the other. He was himself.

Last week his father barged into the bathroom and caught him examining under his armpits for hair. 'A razor for your next birthday, eh, boy?' he had said, but no joking could hide the put down. Mark started to lock doors. Aunt Olga would have made a joke of it, and he would have laughed.

Or the time his mother dragged him around after her, holding the material for the new dining room curtains while she tucked and measured, her mouth full of pins. He felt like a dumbo, and it took so long! He was draped in the floral stuff from head to toe as his mother dropped the second last curtain all over him. She said later she was being playful. Playful! Well, Aunt Olga swept in at that moment and, quick as a flash, she cried out, 'It's the Sheik of Araby, Jennifer, you dark horse! Why didn't you tell me you had your Oriental Lover helping you out so gallantly?'

The women giggled but Mark did not. He scrambled out from under the heavy drapes and shot through, not to his room, but outside where he found the soccer ball and kicked it viciously for half an hour, deliberately aiming at his mother's dahlia bed. Aunt Olga came down in the end and got him out of his mood; she threatened to put lipstick on him, and her rouge – 'though you don't need that with your lovely colouring', she said, just to taunt him. He kicked the ball right at her midriff but she deftly leapt and deflected it sideways with her shoe. He was actually impressed and couldn't help showing it. So they had both ended up in a tussle as she gave him a bearhug and what she called a beating. He loved her more than anyone else in his family.

Why sneak away, then? And to Malaysia? What was she doing there? He could have told her lots of stuff about it, if she had asked him. He had done that project on rubber plantations last year, he still had his assignment book.

And there had been that TV doco on Sabah. He'd wished

he had recorded it on video but you never think of that in time and without the opening credits everything would be lost. Still, he remembered the images of those slender, beautiful Kalantan girls who made even roadwork and hot tar and gravel seem somehow effortless. There had been a sequence with them bathing under a waterfall, too, and with bare breasts. It had been breathtaking and it had stayed in his mind ever since, though it was only a few moments, really. His mother had remarked on what a shame it was to make those girls do all that heavy manual labour, that was a job for men, what were they thinking of? His father had made some comment about the Kalantans being looked down by the Malays, it was all territorial. 'Perhaps it is because the Kalantan are so beautiful?' his mother had said, and Mark agreed.

Would Aunt Olga be going to Sabah? No one told him anything. He could have urged her to go to Kota Kinabalu if she was making a trip to Malaysia. He could have told her about the Kalantans. Sabah was where the main rubber plantations were, too. He would have urged her to go there.

The explanation, when it did come, had been that Olga made the trip on a sudden impulse. She was like that. She had seen a special discount airfare with Malaysian Airlines because of the economic situation and one of her paintings had been sold, the first one in two years, so she decided to splurge on the flight. Uncle Pat hated air travel and besides, he was obsessed with Y2K and all that.

Her flight was on 9.9.99 and Uncle Pat was convinced all planes would drop out of the sky on that day. In fact, dad said, that increased Aunt Olga's fascination with the idea. 'My sister was always like that,' he said. 'She was born on Friday the 13th and I think that made her think she had an affinity with witches and wiccas and wizards. She used to scare me shitless – hmmph – when I was a bit younger than you are, Marcus.'

'Mark,' he murmured, but under his breath.

And he did remember the Friday the 13th party just after his own 13th birthday, last year. Aunt Olga had insisted he come over, alone, no parents, no friends, just himself. And as soon as he opened the door to their cottage he had been bombarded with the full Addams Family stuff, there were even cobwebs, real cobwebs that he had to somehow push through to get inside once he opened the front door. He still felt them tangled in his hair sometimes. And later that evening, after the blood-coloured cakes and the black teeth and the skull that he had to drink black cordial out of and Uncle Pat dressed as a corpulent skeleton in luminous bones, and when he had thought everything was over, and he had gone to the bathroom to clean his teeth, Aunt Olga had insisted he take a bath.

Okay, he said, and when he turned the tap on in the bath the water had come out dark red too. How did they manage that? He had laughed and crowed and Uncle Pat had come in to giggle with him then and had manhandled him out of the last of his clothes and dropped him into the red bath. It turned out to be a bubble bath and the bubbles rose and frothed almost immediately, though the water still felt oily and rather invasively slippery all over his body. Aunt Olga, too, had come in for a laugh at his Hollywood Sex Bath, as she called it. It had been sort of close and intimate but also a bit embarrassing and he was afraid to show what his body was doing down there under the bubbles. He was not like some of the kids at school who swanked round showing their horn in the dressing sheds. 'Stiffie! Stiffie!' they would boast and everybody would laugh. When Aunt Olga laughed at him in the bath he had to join in but rather wished they would leave him alone. When they did, somehow he did not enjoy it that much anyway. The water had grown cold and the bubbles were flattening and only the oily feel all over him remained. Uncle Pat was the last to go and he made much fuss about leaving the big towel for Mark to dry himself on. 'When you are ready.'

That had been the real shock of the night. That towel had been half covered with cobwebs too. Mark had hopped out of the bath and he grinned at the size of it: until he wrapped it round and began drying his genitals. That was when the cobwebs stuck. It was horrible.

He had let out a shriek (and he only realised, later, that his aunt and uncle were just outside the door, waiting for just that moment). He had dropped the big towel instantly, of course, and began rubbing himself hard with the ordinary one that had the blue stripes.

'Just you wait!' he had called, 'I'll put spiders in your bed!' but the very thought of that, and of the possible spiders in his own bed, were enough to stop his gob instantly. He dried himself quickly and dressed again. But he could not lose the sensation of those cobwebs sticking to him, down there, and all over his parts, especially his testicles. He took down his pants once more and rubbed again carefully. No, there was nothing visible. But it felt like it. It was ages before he was able to relax and forget that sensation down below.

They had called him a spoilsport when he said he would go home that night, not stay at their place. Aunt Olga promised on her bended knees that there would be no spiders or cobwebs in his bed or in the bedroom. Uncle Pat brought a hot mug of Milo and promised to sit down by his bed and read him a calming story, like he did once when Mark was a little boy. The story would not be about ghosts and monsters, it would be a fairy story, but an adult fairy story. Mark was an adult now. Uncle Pat had seen that and was sorry he hadn't realised. Aunt Olga said she would paint him, lying in bed and tucked up and wonderful.

He had been appeased.

The story was, it turned out, sort of magical. It was from one of Uncle Pat's own books about a prince who was born grown up and who had to learn how to be a child, which he had never been. The prince did not actually grow smaller or lose those special grown-up things like his body hair and the smell under his armpits, but he realised what he had never had since birth was his innocence. He had been born knowing everything and that had made him unable to love, not even his parents, who were old when he was born and who died soon after. He had grown knowing everything and not feeling anything much because he knew what everything felt like. But one day he saw this beautiful dusky maiden bathing under a waterfall in the forest and for the first time he fell in love, though he knew all too well how love ended up most of the time and he knew what sex was all about, putting his thing in her thing and all that, but he saw this beautiful girl under the waterfall and for the first time he felt that sex was only a small part of what he was feeling. What he was really feeling was the onset of innocence.

'You've got to keep that as long as possible,' his uncle said, and Aunt Olga, who was also sitting alongside the bed, put in, 'innocence means you can still laugh.' She was stroking Uncle Pat's shoulders as he was telling the story so that for the first time Mark felt they had a real closeness together not just the usual joking and sparring and play-acting. He had forgiven them their Friday the 13th silliness and he realised he was not just a victim of their cruel jokes, but had been expected to join in the fun. It was almost as if they had been trying to reinvent their own innocence. Hah! Some innocence! Sticky cobwebs were not Mark's idea of innocence.

When he had come out of the bathroom, still half wet from the haste with which he had dressed himself after the cobweb towel, Aunt Olga had burst into a sort of motherly concern and had insisted he dry himself properly or he would catch a cold. She had stripped off his shirt before he had a chance and had mopped him down. As she rubbed his chest and lifted up his arms she had murmured at how he was developing and he knew instantly she might want to rub the towel vigorously into the crease of his buttocks and mop him all over the tender front parts, but he pulled the towel from her hands and, laughing at last (if secretly out of embarrassment), he said, 'I can do that.' He let her button his shirt again, though. That was when Uncle Pat had gone off to the kitchen for the Milo.

After that new sort of intimacy, things had changed, that was true. He went over to Aunt Olga less often, but when he did he was freer. It was as if they had shared a secret, and it was exciting and very private. His parents would never have understood this newfound intimacy. It was not innocence – it was experience, or the promise of experience.

That was why Aunt Olga's sudden secret flight to Malaysia was so hurtful and so surprising. The intimacy had been ruptured, it was like an assault. Even Uncle Pat, scurrying over to Sydney, seemed part of the conspiracy. Uncle Pat had never been more than a sort of shadow to Aunt Olga, really, but his story telling had opened something up. Mark knew what it was: it had been the first time anyone had told him things about his own body and the grown-up future of his own body in a way that made sense. That preserved the innocence as well as took for granted a great deal about knowingness, and did not make it somehow secret or shameful.

Mark's own father had spoken about sex and masturbation and all that, but the kids at school were there long before that so it was no news. The bits about women and their bleeding and eggs and the pain of having babies, his father had been good on that and it was more urgent, somehow, than the video at school had been. It was as if his dad were confiding real feelings and Mark had asked about his own birth and if it was painful for his mother.

'It was painful for us all,' his father had said, and that had set them both back. It was a new angle on things. 'But I tell you this, son. It was worth it.' And he had given Mark one of his rare cuddles.

Over the next week, while his aunt was overseas, Mark dug up his old essay and assignment book on Rubber Plantations in Sabah. He had forgotten that there was one picture of Kalantan girls working on a stretch of roadwork in the tall forest. He had not noticed before that some of them wore their sarongs so as to free the breasts. Why had he missed that? Not even his teacher had remarked on it. Now that he looked at it again, though, it was quite obvious. He searched out the magnifying glass just to make sure.

And then Aunt Olga was home again. Everything was the same. 'She sweeps everyone before her,' his father said, but he laughed and Mark could see that brother and sister were very close. It came as a jolt. Aunt Olga and his father were so different.

She promised him photographs when they were printed. She had a swathe of batik. She had some little carved wooden figurines and couple of shadow puppets that she was going to save for herself: printed red and gold and with long jointed arms and legs and elongated faces with no upper lips. Mark thought they were just the sort of thing Aunt Olga would go for, both spooky and ridiculous. The male figure was like a cross between a spider and a butterfly. Wayang Kulit, she had said.

But she had brought Mark back a special present. 'I found it in a small village outside Kinabalu,' she said, 'where there was a village madman and those delicate limbed Kalantan girls you've got the hots for, Mark, you randy little monkey. But this is a musical instrument. I think it is called a Selah.'

She handed him a smallish gourd, with a panpipe stuck into it, and a handful of pipes with finger holds. 'You have to puff until you make enough air to fill the gourd and then more so; then you can play several notes at the same time, with those little pipes. I couldn't manage it. But then I could never play the bagpipes either.' She made him try. After the third or fourth attempt he managed to create a small wail on the instrument. That had been enough for both of them.

He took it to school and not even the music master had seen one of these before. Mark did not try playing it again, but it was hung on his bedroom wall, a real trophy. It was only some weeks later that he noticed the telltale signs of some insect infestation. Aunt Olga had smuggled it in past customs.

His father insisted it be destroyed immediately. He snatched it from Mark and took it away to burn, himself.

When Mark went round to tell Aunt Olga of this tragedy, that was when he first saw her latest painting. It was a self-portrait.

'Woman in a red hat,' she called it. It was also the first time Mark noticed how like his own father Aunt Olga really looked. Indeed, when he walked into her studio, which was really the living room of their small cottage, she was eager to show it to him, though often enough she hid her paintings or tore them up. If they were on hardboard she was known to get at them with the axe. She said she could not afford canvas. This one was on paper.

'Wow!' Mark had said. And he meant it.

But he could not get the image out of his mind: it was a picture of his father. Only the floppy red hat made it seem Aunt Olga. It was her hat, he recognised it. That was not sufficient disguise. And the eyes kept staring at him as if they knew. He had never really noticed his father's eyes, but they were his. They were following him and what was really spooky was that the look Aunt Olga had brought into the painting was the sort of look she had that night on the Friday the Thirteenth party. It was the look that seemed to be wanting him to grow up. More, it seemed to be wanting him to take off his clothes so she could reach out and touch him all over. It was Uncle Pat, at the time, who had said 'What a man you are growing, lad.' Aunt Olga, though, had really made him feel how he had changed, in his body, in his mind. It was almost a look of envy, as well as of appraisal. In her painting both his aunt and his father were expecting something of him, something he could not give.

She gave him her painting.

'Perhaps I did it for you,' she said. 'I don't know – anyway, it's yours.'

He thanked her, but he couldn't wait to get home.

The mouth: that had his father's severe look. Eyes and mouth seemed to be saying different stories. When he did have it in his room, Mark could study the painting more closely, and in private. Was all this adult business always so confusing, so filled with conflicting messages and truthful lies? Though he had instantly admired it, now he was not so sure. It was not a portrait of Aunt Olga at all. It did not get her violence or her jokes. Uncle Pat was not in it, and her portrait should have the presence of Uncle Pat somewhere, somehow, if only in the background.

But then he thought of Aunt Olga in Kuala Lumpur or Sabah, alone. And he knew she would be revelling in it. She would be herself then. Like in this portrait.

Those echoes of his father. How could that be? It was as if the cobweb of genetic linkage was a tangled thread, sticky and adhesive, and no matter how you tried you could not get it disentangled. He thought of the feeling in his balls that night. It was still shuddery. It had been days before he had felt, finally, the sticky webs fully removed. He had kept the incident a secret from his father. Perhaps, though, he might have understood. He might even have laughed. Could that be possible? The way his uncle and aunt laughed with him, that was a sort of secret bond, perhaps even a secret promise?

But he did not remark on that reminder of his father in the portrait to his aunt. Instead, he said, 'Have you ever done a painting of Uncle Pat?'

She had laughed. 'Your uncle is too evasive a creature to sit still for a portrait.'

She had drawn out from behind the pile stacked against the wall another work on board. It was the same red hat, but beneath the obscured face the tubby body had something of his uncle's way of lounging over the furniture, though the body was hairless and naked. Indeed, it was like a giant baby's body, even to the unformed genitals. 'He hates it, of course. But he refused to do a life study for me, in the altogether. So I did the next best thing. That's Patrick as he imagines himself to be. This one,' and she pointed back to the newer painting, which Mark had brought over so she could have another look at it, as she said. 'This one is myself as I want people to see me. None of us is ever really honest with ourselves. But you know that, dear Marcus. You, after all, have seen through all of us. Have you forgiven us yet?'

'I haven't forgiven you for sneaking to Malaysia and not telling me.' There, it was out!

His aunt looked across at him but she wasn't smiling now. 'So like your father. So possessive already. Ah, little Marcus, you are growing up, more's the pity.' And her mouth did broaden then. 'Think of all the things I've no intention of telling you. Then ask yourself why?'

She would not be drawn out further. Perhaps no one had been so honest with him before. And he knew he had no way to handle it.

Something had come between them, and it wasn't even honesty. It was like the sweat under his armpits – something new and intrusive. When he left, for the first time he did not kiss her goodbye.

What to Do at the Time

At fifteen it is still possible to be hurt by almost anything. The protective skin has not grown and the quick response still waits until midnight to assert itself. Too late, the enemy has marched off in triumph and timing. At midnight, or 2 a.m. the pillow, now damp with sweat, is more a mockery than a solace; it not only has lumps and hollows, it surrounds your face and thinks of suffocation. It is in the plot, also.

In the other bed, against the fibro partition in the sleepout, Jim is snoring lightly. He means no harm. He is impossible. Jim doesn't seem to feel anything; Jim is the ultimate frustration.

Mick heaves over to his left side and doubles up the pillow to raise his head, see if that will do any good. He knows already this is a vain exercise. He has tried it before. Through the glass louvres there seems to be the promise of a breeze so slight that it does not even stir the leaves of the camphor laurel tree overhanging their side of the house. Mick believes he can feel it, though. He tugs back the damp sheets to let it circulate along his limbs, even though his summer pyjamas stick to him. There is almost a coldness from his eroding sweat, at least for the first minute or two. Both Jim and Mick wear singlets day and night; to absorb the sweat rather than for any protection. Their mother warns them it keeps their white school shirts drier and cleaner. When he unpeels his singlet in the bathroom at night, Mick often senses it is twice as heavy as when he initially tugged it on. Sometimes, in this weather, he has to change his singlet in the morning, too.

Tonight he knows he will twist and squirm and finally drag it off, despite warnings about catching a chill or letting his chest be unprotected. It is Jim, over in his bed, who catches colds and who is vulnerable to asthma, not Mick. For all his stoicism, Jim is the one their mother frets about. Mick can see that easily enough, even though she tries to hide it. No wonder he loses his temper at times; wouldn't anyone? Anyone, except Jim. Mick has already unbuttoned the pyjama top. It, too, is clammy. Summer nights, when the humidity does not drop and the breeze refuses to give even some pretence of coolness, are the worst. The top is off now, and Mick shoves it under the sheet, rather than toss it onto the boards. Now he can get rid of the singlet. He feels its wetness but he rubs it over his smooth chest as if that will mop up the dribble of moisture. This garment is tossed over the side.

Mick does allow the night air to wash over the upper part of his body. It is almost a defiance, secretly disobeying Mum's orders. At school today – yesterday, rather – not only had he failed to win the one hundred metres freestyle but he had let Garth Rasmussen lord it over him in the dressing sheds after, hounding him with a wet towel flick and joking about Mick's white skin where the sun did not get to it. Rasmussen was brown all over and was always skiting about how he went sunbaking with his cousins in the dam back of their place. His girl cousins.

It had got to Mick, not because of his pallid tummy and rear but because Rasmussen kept calling him girly-white, girly-white. Jim always warned his brother about his 'Irish temper'. But Mick had very nearly been dead set to front up to Rasmussen there in the sheds, even though Rasmussen was a good foot taller and built like a tank. It had taken self-control. Mick was good at self-control these days. It had been years since his last turn and he was just a kid then. That whole afternoon locked in the bathroom. He remembered it all right. Of course he remembered, it wasn't his fault.

But Rasmussen was something different. He was deliberately trying to get Mick's dander up. That's why Mick chose to ignore him. Well, almost.

Some of the others had stepped in, but that was not the reason. And it wasn't because Jim had warned him, with that won't-you-ever-learn look of his. The real reason had been that Mick could not think of any retort that would wound Garth Rasmussen.

He had got beyond thrashing out blindly in a temper. He knew in his heart that words were more lethal than hands and arms and going crazy. You must watch that sharp tongue of yours, Mum said. Did she realise that she had made him secretly proud of his wounding way with words? Jim was his first experiment. Well, not experiment exactly; but Jim was always around and that silence of his was always galling. Mick had become the verbal rapier, Dad had said. He was all too aware of that, but it had not helped him in the dressing sheds today. The wounding words had not come. Where was his famous 'sharp tongue' now?

What he really wanted was to brand his enemy with a potent nickname, one that would cling to him like spiderwebs, like his own shadow, to follow him everywhere, long after school, a name that would be so accurate and so cruel Rasmussen would never be allowed to forget it, would never outlive it. One that would replace Garth with a name like Filth, but more clever and more ruthless. It would not matter that nobody might remember who first coined the word, the word itself would take over. There must be such a word.

What was the name that came to him ten minutes ago? Already vanished, now it prods Mick like a finger on his bare chest till he tosses again, and groans, so that Jim over in the other bed raises his head a moment as if awakened, but then collapses back and draws his sheets over his head. He begins snoring lightly, as always; something to do with his nasal cavities, Mum said. Mick stays rigid for a few minutes. He knows there is no hope now; the word has vanished.

Jim seems always to need his bedsheets, even blankets in summer. They have different metabolisms.

Mick, though he might be pallid, has some inner body heat that insulates him whereas Jim would not dream of discarding his singlet, even on a hot night like this is. Mick's chest, though bare now to the air still seems swathed in the surrounding humidity and the dampness swaddles him as if to constrict all volition.

The sheets are tugged right back. He raises his hips and tugs down his pyjama shorts. He looks over to where Jim is sleeping; Jim has turned his face to the wall now and is rumbling quietly; almost with satisfaction, Mick thinks, and feels the usual pang of envy.

Lying naked on the hot bed is to invite the other sensations and Mick knows by this stage he is past caring. He also knows he will feel guilty later, but already the stronger process has begun, and once commenced it has its own inexorability. Does Jim never have these feelings? Mick has never detected any signs. But perhaps Jim is more sly than anything in his character seems to indicate? Perhaps Jim is more subtle? Mick cannot work his brother out, though, being always there, perhaps there is nothing to work out. Jim is who Jim seems: silent, practical, pretty unemotional.

Mick is the one with the highs and lows, the mad, bad feelings and the rages. He is the one who has inherited the Irish genes and Jim comes from some other, stoic line of the family, their father's side.

At a certain point the ears take over, the pulse in your ears reflects the other, mounting pulse and the entire body moves into one single unity, your thoughts then are absorbed into whatever it is that commands you. Then it is done and if you are lucky you will sleep at last. The body discharges itself of tensions; even the night air works with a sort of gentleness to turn sweat into coolness, if only for a short while. Mick does not even remember what it was he had been so restless about.

Garth Rasmussen is not even a shadow in his memory. Jim, over there, breathes on steadily. The luminous dial on Mick's wristwatch is not going to force him to look yet again; the damp feel of his hair against the churned up pillow eases its pressure; he knows he will have to locate those pyjama shorts sometime before morning but not now, not now. He draws the bedsheet up around his shoulders and, though he does not realise it, Mick curls into the foetal position.

+++++

At breakfast Jim is first up and has already piled his plate with four Weet-Bix and is now spreading sugar into hillocks and ridges before inundating the lot with the fresh milk brought in from the milkman half an hour ago. He shaved again this morning and there is a speck of white froth under his right earlobe. He is humming quietly as he pours, probably oblivious that his mouth let anything like musical sounds pass. Jim tends to capitalise on his silence. He didn't wish their parents Good Morning; humming was enough.

Mick enters slowly, rubbing his hands through tousled hair and checking the time on the ornamental clock above the mantelpiece. The wristwatch with its luminous hands and dial was a birthday present last week and he still feels the need to check it constantly. Jim has a watch with a leather protective case, like they use in the air force, he says. It means that he has to unclip it each time he needs to check the time. Mick was at first a little jealous of the neat, professional look of his brother's armpiece but he quickly realised the drawbacks, even though Jim pointed out how useful it was for games like football. Mick does not play football. His glowing numbers and pointers are in some way the product of radiation, he has been told. Radiation kills, Jim quipped. In the dark, though, the glow seems almost magical. Power. Mick couldn't care less about the so-called harm; if it were dangerous, wouldn't they have banned it, or something? Jim has no answer to that. Their father continues to read his paper, over all this quibbling. He is used to it.

Besides, that was last week's issue. Jim now wears his watch with its leather band and cover as if it had grown on his wrist, naturally. Mick's watch has an expanding metal band; it still sometimes catches the hairs on his arm. When it has tugged off all the hairs round your wrist you won't even notice it, Jim had said. Jim's watch does not have an illuminated dial.

Mick sits at the table and his mother brings him two eggs on toast and asks him if he wants some bacon, she has fried some for Dad, she says. Mick hesitates and then says No. When she sits down beside him he asks her if it's today she is going to town with Aunt Meg.

That's clever of you to remember, she says. Your brother asked me to watch his tennis semi-finals but I told him not today, today is the day of the big outing.

I knew it was special, Mick says. You don't hide things from me, you know. I could tell.

She ruffles his already tousled hair and gets up from the table. You really must get your hair cut this week. Both of you, she says, but they know it is only Mick whose mop is so unruly. Jim's hair is straight; a bit of Brylcream and it stays flat all day.

Now you will do your piano practice when you get in, she says. I won't be here to remind you.

As if he needs reminding.

+++++

Lunchtime is the time for his last practice for the Championships, the big ones, and he is determined about the one hundred metres.

Mick is in the pool almost before anybody else and has done three lengths before the next group comes ambling down the slope to the school baths, Garth Rasmussen among them.

Mick concentrates on the task ahead. He always does ten lengths of the pool, to limber up, and then gives himself a rest of five minutes before he gets the school coach, or one of the juniors, to time him for the one hundred. Four, five, six, seven, eight. Garth Rasmussen, he becomes aware, is there in the next lane and he is forcing the pace. Almost without being aware of himself, Mick is keeping up. He is competing. This warm-up swim is not intended for speed, it is for muscular coordination and efficiency. Rasmussen knows that but he is the sort of jock who would compete with his own shadow and then complain that it did not work hard enough. Garth Rasmussen has nothing better to do.

Mick eases back over the last two lengths of his warm-up. He watches Rasmussen do a further two lengths before he pulls up in the adjacent lane and gives Mick a splash. What is it with Rasmussen?

There's another six for you to do yet, Mick tells him, but Rasmussen tugs off his rubber cap. The ash blond hair falls over his face and he flicks it back with a jerk of the neck.

That's your problem, Turner, you always go by the rules. It's not rules that win races, it's cunning. Pity you never learned that one. That's why I'll lick you hollow, see if I don't.

And he throws his cap over the edge and dives back in, even though it has been forbidden to swim bareheaded in the pool, school regulations. Rasmussen's blond hair will turn green, Mick tells himself, and wishes it might be so.

Lined up on the block later, for a last practice, Rasmussen is three lanes distant but Mick knows he might as well be right alongside, his whole body a sneer. Garth Rasmussen might have that golden brown skin, and there are no freckles at all; and he might be a lot taller, and yes, he is built like a tank. But on the other hand, he is not really all muscle, there is some flab you can see from the way his navel dimples and there is already an incipient double chin. Not that anyone minds any of that: Garth Rasmussen has his own band of cronies and is notorious for his handouts of Minties and Jaffas, filched from his auntie's big general store over the other side of town. Rasmussen has a big mouth (in more ways than one, Mick thinks) and very even teeth, like an advertisement, but otherwise why should he have such tickets on himself?

Mick looks round for someone to time him, ignoring Rasmussen who has finished his warm-up session. Jim appears on the scene, his tennis semis must be over (and it is obvious at a glance the results have not been good). Jim and Garth Rasmussen are sort of friends, they are in the same Chemistry and Physics class and sometimes come home together to make what Mick calls stink bombs under the house, while Mick does his piano practice upstairs, getting louder and louder and repeating the scales that he knows drive Jim mad. Scales are the one thing that he can get a rise out of his brother from. Major. Minor. Harmonic Minor. Melodic Minor. Then, because he knows it will really work horrors on Jim, Mick does four octaves of the whole-tone scale. Then he begins the arpeggios. He can do this for hours.

Jim ambles over just at the right moment to be handed the stopwatch from the Prefects' Locker. Jim was butterfly champion last season but tennis has taken him over. Or it had. From the way he gives Mick a glare it is clear that this is not the best day for requests but Mick has no option. He pretends not to notice when Garth Rasmussen steps over beside Jim and moves with him to the pool end. Mick gives his brother a loud warning, and then dives.

There is something compelling about the body in free-style. Water slides along you and the precise arm movements, the regular sideways slant of the body and the paced way the mouth takes breath all combine to make one realise the neatness of speed. Mick's legs, bound together almost, into the kicking rhythm, six to an armstroke for the racing effort, seem to be machines of their own volition, this could go on forever: his first turn at the fifty metres is copybook and he does not need to listen to his brother shouting the number, he knows he is ahead. Ahead of whom? Ahead. Ahead.

At one hundred metres he gauges the arm thrust and hits the end rail. This time he looks up expectantly. Jim lurches over and thrusts out the stilled stopwatch. They smile at each other. It is the first time there is the sense of something shared. But almost at the same moment Rasmussen is also beside them.

Time me now, Turner. That wasn't altogether too bad, young Michael. Now it's my go. Your brother thinks this will be a walkover, Jim, but I've been doing a lot of training up in the dam. Corrie races me. You should see her in Speedos. You should see her without Speedos, but not on your life old sport.

And Rasmussen gives Jim a shove before he leaps up to the starting post, still laughing. Mick pulls himself out of the water but he knows he has to see just how close his enemy gets to his own new record. His mother, last week, called Mick a Water Otter.

It is painful to watch. Rasmussen swims like a porpoise, all over the place, rolling and heaving. But he does have that added length and it isn't all flab in there. He can crack the pace.

Jim gives a shout: for the first fifty metres the two have just about broken even. Mick senses suddenly that his brother might even be hoping that Rasmussen tops him. Would he have been so hearty had he won his own game? Mick separates himself a little from his brother. One of the younger kids comes out with his towel and offers it: Mick gives him a grin of thanks and realises his attention has been diverted.

Diverted long enough to let Rasmussen's pace fall somehow out of his mind. He returns to his brother just in time to note the stopwatch as his brother clicks it immobile. Jim looks up to Mick and wags a finger. There is just one second between them.

Mick can't believe it. He had been sure Rasmussen was already flagging after his fifty metre turn. And the turn itself was all water and splash, too untidy by far, enough to get him disqualified in any reasonable competition. That would never happen here, in this school. And not with Rasmussen. Mick knows he would score on points in any fair competition, but when was competition fair?

That sounds the sort of thing Rasmussen would say.

It will be a good battle, Jim says and crosses over to Rasmussen to give him the news. They crow together, as Mick cannot help noticing.

Keep your mind on the swimming and not on your cousin's Speedos, Jim advises his friend, and they both chortle. It is so unfunny.

Mick had known, absolutely, that he had given of his best. He had done that race against himself, solo in the pool, even if silently in severe competition with the stationery Rasmussen. Every kick had been pure vitriol.

Rasmussen comes up to him then, benign because Jim is near at hand. That was with one hand tied behind my back. As it were. Tomorrow's the real test. And he gives Mick a slap on the back so that it leaves a red mark on his fair skin. There is no way out of this.

Mick towels himself vigorously. He steps into the shower and lets the cold water wash the chlorine smell off. Jim is still laughing with Rasmussen as he strips off and has his own shower, on the other side of the stalls. At one point he looks over at Mick. He seems almost embarrassed. Mick cannot help it that his skin is so pale. So pale and so freckled where the sun bites it. He took up swimming because it was a way to get into the sun and the water with some purpose; he had thought it would help that look, like a peeled potato, which has been with him for life. Jim and his olive skin: he can stay out in the sun all day and it never matters. Mick has only ever seen someone else as pallid as himself: when Johnny Armstrong came to the school from down in Melbourne, last year. It is terrible to be embarrassed by oneself.

Two of the other boys come in. That was a good cracking pace, Turner, one of them says. Wish I could manage that just for the fifty metres.

Nah, his friend says, Turner's the white seal, you're the pet cocker spaniel. And they both set to with their towels. Mick pushes through their maelstrom and heads for the clothes pile. Jim and Garth Rasmussen are still talking in the showers, about girls and whatever else causes Jim to laugh so blatantly. It is not like Jim at all.

Mick feels even more vulnerable. Why should that be?

+++++

The last of Mick's 'wild Irish' fits was the worst. Mick remembers it because he can still feel, somewhere deep inside, the outrage and overriding fury of that outrage, when he discovered Jim had meddled in his clothes' drawer – Mick's drawer, the second from the top – and had taken the special packet of transfers Aunt Aggie had saved from her cereal packs and handed to Mick when he called over with the chokos from Dad's garden. Mick had hidden them under his hankies, thinking they'd come in useful sometime.

Jim, without asking, simply took them and used them on his balsawood planes. He had built six of them, they were his pride and joy. He had varnished four and was waiting for new transfers of Air Force emblems for the others. Mick tore downstairs, two at a time, and crashed open the gate to the downstairs work room where Jim kept his models and his unfinished planes. He thumped Jim over the back with both fists, then pounded him over the head where Jim was sitting. Before even screaming out his rage Mick swept the finished models from their shelf, breaking them, and would have picked up the chisel from the bench if Jim had not been quick enough. Mick had the advantage but Jim had the precision. Mick ended up pushed to the concrete, kicking and flailing as Jim finally pinned him down, after much effort; though Mick's strength in these outbursts was almost unnatural. Jim had learned a few tactics of his own, and he had the merit of cool-headedness.

He felt misunderstood.

+++++

It is two days later; the morning of the swimming championships. Jim is clearly nettled that their parents have promised to be there. They did not turn up for his tennis contest. Just as well, he thinks but that does not really help. Mick, as usual, manages to be centrestage. Jim eats his four Weet-Bix stoically and shuts up. When his mother asks him about the chemistry test he grunts. He rises from table just as Mick comes in, sluggish as usual. He pulls the pud too much, and that's the truth. No self-control at all. One day Jim will have his own separate room. Even if he has to leave home to do it.

Good luck today, Mick, Jim grunts as he whips out his bicycle clips and heads off. Mick looks up and gives a smile, almost of gratitude.

But at the lunchtime break, just before the races begin and the people are allowed into the school grounds for the contest, Jim, who has been uncharacteristically grumpy all morning, not his usual self-contained self, gets involved in a stupid argument with one of the kids. It is not even someone he has much to do with.

If I had a brother like Mick Turner I'd get some brown boot polish and polish him up; he's so white it makes you sick, Colin Thompson had said.

That was it. Jim grabbed him by the scruff and pushed him against the big jacaranda by the tennis courts.

What's that you said about my twin?

Can't you take a joke? Why are you and him such different colours, but? Suss to me, that is. Very suss.

Jim was into him and even he was surprised by the vehemence. It took Garth Rasmussen to break in and intervene and even then Jim turned on him and they ended in a wrestling match on the lawn, almost within sight of the Headmaster's upstairs verandah. It became a real fight.

Mick heard of it from one of his classmates. He rushed around and found Jim sprawled under Rasmussen and still struggling.

Something like a white sheet of fury entered Mick's spirit then. He threw himself on Rasmussen, fists gripping and with a strength that clearly took Rasmussen unprepared, surprising him with a force that unbalanced him and left him sprawling. Jim, released, started to pick himself up.

Mick had to be forcibly restrained by two or three of the onlookers. His freckled face was flushed deep red and his eyes were almost unseeing in their wildness. They were frightening.

Rasmussen began laughing, awkwardly, as he dusted himself down and stood up to resume the conflict – with whichever of the brothers chose to be in it. Both, if necessary.

But that was quickly avoided. Let your brother fight his own battles, one of the boys hissed to Mick. You two can't gang up like that, let him finish where he started off. It was his fight. And Mick was shaken by several arms gripping his shoulders, to make sure he heard what was being said.

Slowly he nodded, and then pulled back.

Quick! Teacher! One of the others whispered. They all dispersed into separate parts of the yard and Mick was led away by some of the other members of his swimming squad. He was still shaking with something of an echo of that rage, the madness that claimed him and took over, like the times he was a kid, before he learned.

He had found himself fiercely protective in a way he had not been prepared for. That image of Jim sprawled, on the ground, straddled over by Rasmussen and struggling to get free: what you do at the time of your first emergency is not quite what you might have anticipated, nevertheless what you do is absolute ground base. It is what matters.

Mick had never thought of his twin in those terms. He had never even asked himself (why should he?) what really matters.

He looked over to seek out his brother. Jim and Rasmussen over there, laughing together, chiyacking each other.

Mick turned away. No. It's no surprise. That deep rage which spurred him into action had been self-generated, no doubt about that. And yet, no, not self-generated, it was something quite outside self.

He walked up to them and they quietened down.

He caught Garth Rasmussen's eye and held it. You lay a finger on my brother, I'm telling you, you'll have me to contend with. Like you say, Rasmussen, it's cunning that counts, and once I start nothing can stop me.

Aw, Mick. Come off it, Jim attempted to intervene.

Once you get me going, you will regret it, Gat Ratmutton, ask Jim, he will tell you; Mum calls it the wild Irish but if I get started I can't stop. So don't get me started, Ratmutton.

Now Mick ... His brother attempted a laugh but nobody was convinced. They were all waiting.

You tell him, Mick repeated When I was twelve that time you all thought I'd gone out of control. Out of control, that was what Dad said, but I was a machine then, I was a machine.

Not here, Jim whispered. Mick, you're getting yourself worked up ...

Too right I am. But I'm telling you, Ratmutton, I can be subtle, too, I can play my own jokes if I have to; remember the salted Weet-Bix, Jim? Remember that time?

Jim looked almost grateful. His brother had somehow defused himself, that frightening head of steam had been prevented from building up. When was it, two years ago? Jim knew his brother's eye was no longer fixed onto Garth Rasmussen. Jim played back the opening.

Not the week of the salted Weet-Bix! he exclaimed with such unexpected vehemence that everyone broke up. Jim Turner was not noted for dramatic acting; that was his brother's line. They all wanted to know more, and even Mick ended up laughing and explaining.

Jim let his brother move back centre stage.

Every morning, regular as the milkman's horse, Jim has these four Weet-Bix. Mick gave a wink to his brother. You can time him, too. Quarter to eight on the dot – pick up the Weet-Bix packet, shove out four Weet-Bix. Reach for the sugar bowl. Three big spoonfuls of sugar, over the Weet-Bix. Pour in the milk – from the side, never on top. Let the milk seep up the dry sides and when the sugar begins to melt and not before, then Jim shoves in his spoon and the swishing and dunking begin. It is 7.48 exactly by then. I've timed it. Regular as clockwork.

Mick's always running late, his brother put in.

Weet-Bix, sugar, and then milk. In that order. Every time. What would happen, Jim, if you put the milk in before the sugar? I've even suggested Jim put the milk in first, like an ocean to float his Weet-Bix in. You think he's interested?

Only Mick would suggest milk in first. He's got no sense of order.

Well, I decided something had to be done, before Jim turned into clockwork himself. I got up early before piano practice and I filled the sugar bowl with salt. No one saw me.

But didn't your parents …?

Dad doesn't have cereal and Mum always waits till we're finished. Jim is always first with the sugar bowl. In this case, with the salt bowl.

But you can tell the difference. You can feel it.

At 7.48 am? Jim didn't give it a thought.

That's true. Not at first.

Until he took his first mouthful.

Ugh! I'll get you for that, Mick. I'll think up some revenge, just you wait.

I'll help you, Garth Rasmussen said. Who could endure salt on his Weet-Bix? What a sacrilege to a Weet-Bix. What did it taste like, Jim?

But Mick gave his brother a bear hug. Jim's making deep plots, I know. Will my stamp collection be safe? Or has Jim hidden plans to short-sheet my bed and sprinkle it with pepper? Tell you this, salt Weet-Bix, once tasted never forgotten.

Mick's black rage seemed as if it had never existed it had evaporated so completely. Jim looked on, hands in pockets, his fingers rubbing bruised knuckles against the tight cloth.

+++++

They all ended up in a gang making down to the races. Mick in the centre and Jim more or less quietly mingling with the others. Not with Garth Rasmussen either. He remembered being under him, and carried his own quiet feelings of unforgiveness.

It was, in fact, Jim who insistently spread the tag name of Ratmutton till it became currency, at least for that year.

Mick himself was looking forward to the big race, almost upon him. It did not matter, now, that when he stood on the blocks, his tight belly and muscly buttocks under the Speedo racing togs were pale as a peeled potato, or a white seal.

Turkish Coffee

Dragana had already cleaned all the sauce from her plate of pasta. She had broken the bread with relentless fingers. 'Only a light meal, a small salad,' she had said when they first sat down. Rachel was still using her fork to divide the pale, dry sections of gemfish. These looked – and tasted – like string. Something out of the deep freeze. But almost anything she tried, today, would seem tasteless.

Dragana with sharp eyes scanned the crowded Italian restaurant. They were squeezed at a small table alongside the major party, twenty birthday celebrants, everyone in black. It was a very Melbourne function, the men swarthy and the women elegantly coiffed. Dragana's suit was plum coloured, the waist nipped in with a conscientious neatness that betrayed its origins.

'Do you know I was in Belgrade in March? The twenty-fourth of March, when the Americans began their bombing. Yes, I was there, and only halfway through my research; I would be there now.'

'How did you escape?' Rachel's interest was aroused. She had met Dragana only twice before. A mutual acquaintance, the formidable Ortrun, had declared Dragana a fire-breathing monster. Rachel was of course impressed. Anyone who challenged Ortrun had to be, at the least, estimable. Dragana, tonight, was all smiles and constant, if firm, chatter.

'I should be in Belgrade still. But we crossed the border

into Hungary and went up to Budapest. Two weeks after the bombing started. I am from Belgrade. I was born in Belgrade, so I felt these things.'

More Italians had arrived at the long table, more than there was seating for. The newcomers were also young, or youngish, and in black. The women's smiles were magnificent, their hair sleek and even more magnificent. Two of the young men, closest to Rachel, had at least four rings on each hand, heavy gold. She imagined gleaming medallions on golden chains rubbing their dark chest hair, but tonight silk ties were tight to the neck; and arms, in their expensive suits, sprawled everywhere, sometimes impeding the waiters. How they carry all that flamboyance, she thought. Such unself-consciousness. She was a real sucker for that. She fell for it every time. And yet, beneath those well-tailored suits, they were probably only boys. But they all looked so young these days; she must not be critical.

The most expensive items from the *primi* were most popular: giant king prawns and the Moreton Bay bugs. Rachel carefully placed her knife and fork in a parallel flank among the discarded gemfish shreds and the steamed carrot and broccoli. She reached for the wine bottle and replenished Dragana's goblet.

'Now. Yourself. What have you been doing?' But the waiter appeared with the Dessert selection before Rachel could reply and Dragana was instantly declaring her intentions. 'This ice cream? What are the three flavours? I will not have chocolate, but if you have three flavours without chocolate, that is what I will have. And a little cream. Then, as a finish, give me the short black coffee. I always have a Turkish coffee at home but that is not expected here, so I will have a short black. And you, Rachel, have you chosen?'

There was a time when Rachel had almost invented Turkish coffee for herself. It was a drug. Then she had tasted real Turkish coffee in Istanbul. She had returned to Australia bearing a large brass samovar, two prayer rugs and an even more passionate taste for genuine Turkish coffee.

In time she had settled for Nescafe Espresso, but that was many years later. Many many years later, and the incident of the fortune teller no longer reminded her so insistently.

It is funny how the mind censors many things, how the past remodels itself in accordance with present predilections. It is as if we take what we will, or what we remember, out of a grab bag of memories with all the skill of a juggler, whose very art is not only precision, but deception. Everything must appear to be more difficult than it is. Everything must appear easier, almost a gift. Everything is on the surface. Everything is hidden.

That was where the fortune teller rankled. Rachel was not really filled, ever, with the trickeries or the difficulties of Turkey. She had, before that wonderful expedition, read her guide books and her histories. She was not one to stride down a bazaar wearing a short summer dress and sandals. Long flowing robes were infinitely more delightful and she knew she could never attempt them back in Brisbane. She wore heavy necklaces and amulets, earrings and bulky finger rings. She bartered with gestures and fingers and all the primal numbers in Arabic, which she had memorised while waiting for three hours at Bahrain airport. She knew when to walk away and when to throw up her hands. It was with infinite sadness that she finally accepted the penury of the stall holder and graciously consented to accept his trinket for a ridiculously small exchange of coins.

When she had made her one big killing – the samovar – that was the time she sat, graciously, on a cushion and carpet bestrewn divan and accepted her first Turkish coffee, sur-rounded by the two gentle old men and the excited clutter of little boys, all of them huge eyed and serious.

She was told the history of the large vessel, its antiquity

and its provenance, though she only caught the one signifi-
cant word – Suleyman – and she examined the pale markings
with genuine interest and thought of the slaves and harems
and giant eunuchs with servile hands.

The fortune teller materialised out of nowhere, or out of
the milling crowds, who paused, moved, jostled and flowed all
around her. The old men were evidently delighted to see her
and she was given a place of veneration almost as reverently
as that accorded to Rachel. The old woman motioned for her
to finish her coffee. Rachel drained the dark sandy-textured
dregs, wiped her mouth with the white handkerchief jammed
into the amulet on her plump right arm, and looked, herself,
into the murky depths of the tiny white cup, before handing
it across to the eager brown fingers.

'You speak English?' The old woman had a tobacco voice
that reminded Rachel of her own Aunt Dolly – the 'fast' one
who had become wealthy in Potts Point. It was both a relief
and a little annoying to find herself so promptly identified.
She had not uttered a word during the entire negotiations,
the bartering, the careful wrapping or the courteous invitation to coffee and this opulent interior of the small market-
place tent. At no point had Rachel felt the slightest hesitation
or nervousness. She was prepared for anything, but not even
her moneypurse, hidden beneath the flowing garments, had
seemed in the least threatened. The fortune teller was tiny,
wizened, and in her smoky voice, at one stroke, she exposed
her. Rachel knew her bulky necklace had already been
assessed and valued, the one turquoise ring among the pretty
other baubles immediately noted, and she hoped the cynical
twist at the corner of her mouth had been properly identified.

The old woman reached out her other hand before
gazing, herself, into the proffered coffee grounds, and took
up Rachel's turquoise finger. She looked into her eyes then,
just for a moment though it seemed endless. Rachel knew not
to waver.

'Yes, you speak English, but you are not England.' She waggled the finger in her own grasp. 'You come to Istanbul to find love, yes?'

Rachel had spluttered. The spell was broken.

'I came here for … for …' But the words, surprisingly, had not come. She could have said 'for adventure', or 'for the sense of history,' or even 'for the excitement of a world where I do not know the rules and where my wits must carry me.' But it had never crossed her mind to use the word 'love' in any of its contexts.

She clutched the large samovar in her arms, as if it were the demonstration of her reason for being here.

The old woman saw. She nodded and grinned, revealing an almost full set of strong teeth, yellowish but decisive. 'You have found your love, then. It will please you, but you will have dryness in your mouth.'

Then she finally took up the tiny cup and looked for a long while closely at the black dregs. Despite her disbelief, Rachel could not hide her interest or her curiosity. The boys by now had all gathered round and were craning, too, to examine the contents. The two old men sat back and waited. They had all day.

'You wonder I speak the English?' the old woman said. 'It is because of the war. I was young in the war, you will not believe how big my eyes were in the war, how big my hunger for everything. Words. Meanings. They were men, all those boys. They taught me and I taught them. The English. Then the New Zealand boys and the Australians. I was in Wellington two years, do you know that? You, you are not England, you are Wellington, or is it Sydney?' She laughed, a sound like paper being ripped, or parchment. 'You see, I know everything about you.'

Rachel had been prepared for the well-documented strategies of fortune tellers – the quick observant eyes, the conversational scratching of tiny offguard revelations, the adept analysis of apparel, clothing like a personal definition that classifies everyone. She had felt complacent, aware that no other Australian would wear with such generous flair her 'bazaar khaftan' as she liked to call it. She had walked out of the pensione that morning encased in her own sense of exoticism and theatrical pizzaz. What had given her away? What had betrayed her?

The fortune teller's silence and concentration held the whole crowd spellbound. Rachel had leaned forward, too, despite the cynicism.

'It is so.' The old woman finally muttered. 'Look, see!' But she had whisked the tiny bowl too quickly under Rachel's eyes and now was staring at it again herself, fully in control. 'You are a strong woman. But that will not protect you.' She turned then and spat, accurately, onto the one small area of sand outside the tent flap, some three feet distant. 'It never protects you.'

And it was at that moment that Rachel realised, with some genuine disappointment, that the old woman was more an autobiographer than a prophet, a teller of futures and fortunes. It would have been enjoyable, in this rich and truly exotic context, to have been offered a magical formula, something she could joke about later but remember.

It would be nothing but some old habits of mind from this old woman, practicing her English on the first comer, no doubt delighted to have spotted her prey, and indeed accurately to have assessed Rachel's origins. No doubt it had been something she noted from afar, like her walk, her stance, the cast of her shoulders and forearms in motion, that had identified her. Rachel, herself, had picked out Aussies in Venice only last month, just by the way they lounged and lurched in a crowd from the Vaporetto.

'You are strong, though, and there will be many good moments. You are marked for a rich life. There are children. Yes, there are children. Children are always a joy and a disappointment. They are balls of wool. They should be neat and perfect but they always unravel. You want to know how many children? I cannot tell you that. Do you think of children?'

But Rachel, whose life to that point had been crammed with ambitions and plans and a whole Atlas of opportunities or possibilities, had never had the slightest inkling of children. Her sister's infant shat in her lap, once, and Rachel decided on the spot that it is not necessary to suffer everything. There are choices. Rafe was around at that stage, too, and Rafe's definition of 'choice' was another of the more arcane of the maps on their shared atlas. They had booked on the same liner to Rome, though after that first week with Rafe and his new friend Orlando, Rachel had been happy to launch out on her own. She, not Rafe, had been the *cicerone* on that first week. She had memorised all the itineraries and, perhaps for the first time, had realised how retentive and accurate her own memory was. Rafe had been content to let her lead. That had been another bone of contention. And besides, Orlando had been the one to complain incessantly of weariness. He could not manage a cathedral without endless pauses, much less one of the thoroughgoing galleries.

'And who is the father of these children of mine?' she had asked airily. 'Do the coffee grounds tell you that? I would be curious to know,' she added, aware that the old fortune teller would be already making assumptions.

'That, I think, is for you do decide. Yes. That is something you will decide. But believe me, the children are there and they will not be denied their entrance into this world of sorrow and pain.' She gave a sharp nod, one of the children instantly snatched the coffee cup from her hands and disappeared. The old men moved forward. Rachel knew this was the moment and that she must not fudge it. The coin she fumbled from the pocket of her khaftan (Pockets! Such useful receptacles!) was suspiciously generous looking, but it must do. She sailed out of the tent bearing her samovar and did not even look behind at the old woman, though surely there must have been some arrangement, some commission, some form of licence or exchange. Her part in the scenario was done. She found herself without the heart to enter into further barterings or negotiations with the sellers of slippers or the merchants dealing in bronze or leather. For the first time, ever, she was convinced, she had been implanted with the idea of children.

In the Trattoria Rustica on Lygon Street the crowded table just behind Rachel and Dragana had become noisy, toasts were beginning, and all the young people had relaxed out of their elegance into more argumentative or amorous positions. Coats had been flung over the backs of chairs, at least one of the girls had strands of hair that were not part of a conscious gamine presentation, and for the first time Rachel noted the bloke at the head of that table – he had a black and white hide jacket showing now which must have been previously hidden by his expensive Italian suitcoat.

It was vulgar and debonair, cheeky in its way but decidedly placing him in that company as being both egotist and vulnerable, his wide shoulders and the almost Valentino moustache and sideburns reinforcing the assertiveness and the loud extroversion that was dangerously close to innocence, so that she glanced immediately at the other members of that party, and decided that he was perfectly at home and that not one of them saw his gaudy outfit as being other than himself. He was that sort of person. She had a sudden flash of memory. How old would Benno be now?

She turned to her companion. 'Dragana, do you notice that young man over there, the one in the cowboy waistcoat, it's like a bolero. Yes, that's the one.'

But Dragana glanced and turned back without a nod. 'They're all Macedonians,' she said. 'We call them cowboys.'

'I thought they were Italian.'

Dragana gave her a level look. 'How long, Rachel, since you were last overseas? No, I do not mean that American trip, which was when we first met, in L.A. Didn't you once tell me you had been for a week in Istanbul?'

'Twenty five years ago. I tremble to think what has been done to that beautiful old city.'

'You would not want to go back. I almost do not want to go back to Belgrade. My husband is a Croat you know. This last time, from the start, had its small upsets but you cannot allow such things to prevent your plans. Look at that girl near the end. No, not so obviously. You see? Nowhere in Italy would you see bones like that, except among refugees. Oh, perhaps up in Trieste, but that is hardly Italy. We had our honeymoon in Trieste. The wind blew constantly, from every angle.'

Rachel was thinking of Istanbul, though, and of how she deliberately missed her plane that time. She had not found love, but there had been her brief intoxication, as she was later to call it, with proper irony. Benno had been born in Brisbane. For sixteen years he had absorbed her utterly, that was true enough. She stole another look at the young man, but turned her attention to the crepe in front of her. She had allowed it to get cold.

When Benno had decamped it had been a relief. Simply that. Benno knew every art of blackmail and he used each one. She had not initiated any panic search. It was almost as if she, herself, was the one who absconded. Two can play at games, she had said to herself, then or sometime later. She took a position in Melbourne. She did not pick up the pieces, she allowed them to drop away into whatever nooks and corners. It was always refreshing to start with a clean slate and she had done precisely that.

Dragana hailed the waiter. 'Now. We are ready for coffee. Ah, is there a place nearby where it would be possible to have a Turkish coffee? No, I am not serious. You see, in the end,

I am always a creature of compromise.' She took two sips of her tiny cup and looked up at Rachel. 'So. You have organised your whole life? Commendably?'

'Commendably.' Rachel smiled at the expression. 'Yes. I think I have organised my life commendably. I've had a lot of practice, as it were. But do you know, I can't get that young man at that table out of my sight. Do you know what it is? He reminds me of my son. Of how my son might be, at that age.'

'Really? I did not know you had a son, but why not? Where is he now?' Even Dragana could not hide the implication and the suggestion. She angled and fished but could not get Rachel to say more. 'Well, you are a close one. I like that. Come. I must write up my notes. The next conference is in Toronto. You must make the effort to get there. It is commendable also to expose oneself to chances and risks I think. Like in Belgrade in March. Oh, we took our risks all right. But when it happens, sometimes life does overtake. Then it is commendable to make a quick exit.'

She gathered her things and raised her hand to her captive waiter. 'My husband speaks of children, but there is no time. I do not want to raise a child in Belgrade.' She shrugged.

Rachel reached into her purse. She could not avoid the feeling that Dragana was being patronising. But she had learned to settle for that.

As she walked to her car, alone, she was thinking, again, of the brash young man with his black hair and his too willing smile. Those sturdy shoulders. Slowly she imagined him stripping off his clothes, it was like a scene from some forgotten movie or an imagined, or unimagined, past. The setting was a hot hotel in Istanbul. She could afford to be indulgent.

As a boy Benno had been charming, and wilful, and imperious. He had gauged her weakness for the strong, black coffee and when he wanted something he would brew it for her – pungent, fragrant. She would not have it any other way. But that was before he became unmanageable and could smell his freedom. Well, she too had lit out. One must never become dependent. She had organised her life, yes, commendably. Children, after all, are only a loan.

This was the first time in many years she had seen somebody who so strongly conjured up his image, or his possibility. Yes, she thought. The old Gypsy fortune teller had been right. There was still a dryness in her mouth. But a mother is allowed only such a tiny sip out of the coffee cup, and all the rest, at the bottom, is the grit of bitter grounds.

Pristina

Because my grandfather said the water here was still in a pristine state, that's why. He called his property Pristina and the little settlement that sprang up round the crossroads naturally took the same name. Grandpa owned all that land originally. Or at least he leased it; same thing.

Well, the Wayfarer's Inn was the first, where the Sportsman's Motel is now. Their pub on the main street, well that's recent. Relatively. They're still Irish, been here almost as long as us. But they did work hard, give them that. The lot of 'em and the womenfolk most of all. Drank the profits, but. Though Mickey, he's my age, you wouldn't believe what a tough little bugger he was. He was the backbone of the district soccer team, before the grog of course. Yairs, we had some good times back then, if you think of it.

Then there was the Post Office store. I tell you what, people today just take everything for granted but when that store opened – it was before my time, and yours – we knew Pristina was on the map. My old man got married the same year – 1923 – and he said all his birthdays had come at once, that's what he said. He got the property too, very same year. Grandpa had his first stroke; Dad always said it was the excitement, but whatever, Dad was running the place from then on. No one would believe the old man would hang on another forty years. Now who could believe that? Yairs, I remember his room out in the back shed. Well, corrugated iron outside. Outside, mind you, but Dad had it lined. He did it himself, he told me, with knotty native pine. It still smelled strong when I was a kid, that pine, but it was snug as a big bug in there and I remember old Grandpa writing on his little pad to say he didn't mind the dark. His eyes, you see. And he listened to the radio, all the time he listened: Parliament, the races, the news; he followed the news.

Yairs, I remember him well, the old codger, though it was hard to think of him as he was in the old photos: that stiff white collar and tie. And the gloves. Do you know he had gloves in those old photos? Well, times change.

But the pub and the Post Office store, they were only the start. With the second pub, right in the centre, we knew we were there. The government took back some of Dad's land, the scrappy stuff out towards the Magic Mountain. Well we always called it the Magic Mountain, it's only on maps you see the official name: Cable Top. Well, it's true, all those new people call it Cable Top nowadays but they don't count. Not really.

No, I'm not saying that. I'm telling you how things were. How things got settled and established, how this place got its name and its character. It's real character, not this later rot.

The Verralls too, don't forget the Verralls, though there's none of them left in the district, but they were big in the district, oh for ages. And the Weatherheads of course, Mum was a Weatherhead. They were great farmers, the Weatherheads, they introduced the irrigation and the new crops – peanuts, for instance, and then in the war, the Second World War, they took up the government plan for cotton. For a few years there they made a fortune on cotton. And the cannery, it was their cannery – until it was bought out by Yates, that is. Yes, Grandpa Weatherhead was a genius in his way. I think it was him brought out the first reffos, after the war.

When the cotton was big he used a lot of Italian POWs to do the hard yakka. Cheap as dirt they were, he said, and grateful for anything. That was what gave him the idea later, when he opened the cannery and put in the irrigation and began growing miles, simply miles, of carrots and beetroot and all those beans. For canning. He organised a whole tribe of reffo Balts: Yugoslavs, or Croats or Albanians, no they weren't Greeks, and they had their own religion so they certainly were not Reds. No way. They were escaping all that.

And work! Grandpa Weatherhead had a real nose for these things, and you should have seen the way they worked for him. They would have tilled the fields with their bare hands, give 'em half the chance.

And he treated them well. They were their own slaves, not his. He gave them holidays on their religious feasts, that sort of thing. Enough to keep 'em happy, he said, but not enough to give 'em ideas.

That is true, yes it is. Pristina had the first kebab house in Australia. More a backdoor business to start off, that flat bread. And they kept goats and sheep, almost from day one. I remember we kids – well, I was in my teens then – we used to sneak down and cadge some of those flat bread rolls with meat in them. Tell the truth, I think that was what gave some of them the idea in the first place. Before you knew it, they had taken over the little bakery that was shut down when the new sliced bread came in, it was right near the pub, and before you could say Jack Robinson they were out and away.

I always said it was the Kebab House and not the new branch of the Bank of New South Wales that gave the place its little economic boost in the late fifties early sixties. Aha, we thought we were made in those days.

Well, it was the commercial travellers, see. You think on it: you get sick of pea and pies in the pub, or some dry white bread with ham and sweaty cheese, and those blokes weren't the ones to stop for a steak and eggs in the Greek cafe and they couldn't afford to linger over too many beers, not in those years when the competition was really hotting up. No, the Kebab House struck gold.

We didn't get Chinese or Pizza Huts, or even Kentucky Fried, oh that was decades later.

Well of course they did spread out, but Grandpa Weatherhead always said that was the sign of his success; they didn't move on after the first few years, into the city or the easy fleshpots or the mixing pots down south.

They kept their own community, that's what he said. And he was right. Most of the original lot he brought over stuck together, and didn't they work hard! I think they ended up bringing just about their whole village over, in time. Yes, they spoke their own lingo among themselves, and that was a problem as you say, you know how country people suspect others of talking behind their back, and in a foreign language that didn't go down well.

But the kids went to the local school – in fact, because of the increase in numbers we got a second teacher and then a third and it became quite a centre. And then when young Ibrahim showed us all from the outset what a soccer champ he was, or had the potential to be, that was a real turning point, I think.

Well, the Irish clans all got onside with them and before you knew it it was soccer, soccer all the way. I used to play League myself when I was a kid but by the early 1960s League was dead in this town. We were soccer all the way. It was a real cultural revolution.

Broke down barriers, I think you'd say. Strange, it was only the family that ran the Greek Cafe who stayed stand-offish. Oh, unhygienic, all that sort of stuff. Even had the city health inspector round one time, complained of flies and vermin in the Kebab House, but everyone knew they were business rivals. The nice ending of that story, though, is that the Kebab House was the first to install one of those blue-light electric zappers in their shop. While the Greeks and the people in the pub were still using those sticky flypaper things, you remember those? Well, everybody forgets.

So, that was a sign of how they were going money-wise. They kept a low profile, though, those years. I think it was the first generation thing. They knew their origins and their village or their farming backgrounds.

It was in the next generation, really, back in the seventies, when I think you can pinpoint the beginnings of all the trouble.

Young Ibrahim was the first. I think we all thought he'd go national, or even international, with his soccer success. People were just beginning to pay money to get stars on their team, but no. Ibrahim married the girl he had grown up with and he settled right in town. In the village, I mean. I think he was the first to actually buy a piece of land. Even the Kebab House was done on a lease; yes, we owned all that side of the street.

Two things I think we didn't expect. First, that when they bought the O'Reilly farmlet just over the Willowtree Bridge, we assumed they would move into the little cottage there, it was big enough for starters. Second, after they ripped that pretty little place down, and all the garden beds old Doss O'Reilly spent her lifetime pruning and patting and planting, lo and behold, they put up this ugly fortress thing, like a prison compound – it's still there, people take it for granted now, but when it first went up it caused a near riot, I can tell you.

I think that was the first time anyone really got the sense we had been invaded.

No, I'm not putting it too bluntly, that's what people think. That's what we really think here, those of us who remember the old days.

You've seen the other farms too, no doubt. The compounds. The place is full of them, they're everywhere. Miles around. All built the same way: big fences around the house and the house yard, eight feet high some of them, what's that in the fancy new measurement? And the buildings themselves, some of 'em have bars on the windows have you noticed that? They say it's to keep the girls in, they're very heavy on keeping their women under lock and key, a bit like the Italians up in Innisfail, though of course you've heard stories too, I bet you have, isn't that true? It's all a front, but they're not joking I'll tell you that. There have been a few nasty incidents over the years, over the past few years.

Well that's true, in more recent times it has gone over the odds, but we'll get to that. What I was telling you was how it all sort of grew on us, almost so we didn't notice. Woke up one morning, and there they were, trying to run the place, acting as if they owned it.

When young Ibrahim went on the local Shire Council I think we all gave a bit of a cheer and that's the truth. Good to see a local make good. Good to see the lad show some civic spirit also, he was a hard worker, that one. And at that time nobody could have foreseen that I'd be the last of our line, and of the Weatherheads too, I'm the very last one.

My kids, when they went to the University down in the capital, well I knew the professions were the way to the future, the drought years and the flood years come in cycles but they come all right and both my sons said they were jack of that. Don't blame them, really.

And of course the three girls never intended to stay up here, out of it all; their mother made sure of that and they knew perfectly well Roger and Tim would inherit the place. If they wanted it. Only Nessie ever grumbled and whinged about her share and it's true, I had a soft spot for her and I guess I had led her to expect some part, after all she was the only one came back willingly on holidays, right from boarding school, and seemed genuinely interested in things. She was mad on horses, that one.

But she was the one who nagged me into the irrigation, while I was still dithering about the cost. Best investment I ever made. Her mother always said she was more a

Weatherhead than the Weatherheads but she was my secret favourite.

Oh, the boys did all right for themselves, all of that. But I'll still remember the way they mooched around the homestead those last holidays, couldn't get them out into the sun even, the pair of them.

Tim's high in one of those accountancy agglomerates now, I suppose you know that. Spends half his life in Singapore, hope he finds it fun, I didn't the one time I was there. Yes, Roger's the one with the dental practice on the Gold Coast, oh rolling in it.

So I was telling you about Ismael Ibrahim in that dirty big compound of his. That's what I called it, a compound. And if you'd've seen his wife when she was young you wouldn't believe how pretty she was. Petite, you know, and those big black eyes. Well, after fourteen kids, yes that's what I said, after fourteen of them, one each year like the Irish used to do, well who'd recognise her now. Hard as nails she is, she was the one that beat me down – not him – over the block of shops in the side street; she fair wore me down, and I still don't know how she knew before I did about Caffertys Coaches and their planned interstate comfort stop right in the village centre. Beat me down forty per cent on my asking price AND I thought I'd got a bargain, they'd all been empty since the newsagent shot through owing me rent on the corner one, and that would have been two years before. Well, will you look at them now!

No, I don't hold that against them. Not really. And after all, the other block of mine on the main street has done very well out of the Caffertys Coaches and their stopover. Real money spinner, matter of fact. And my god, she is a hard worker, though the whole tribe are out there like a pack of demons, day and night almost.

1970 I think it was, but a lot can happen in the space of a decade or so.

I think it was only when Tim came up here with his kids two years ago that it dawned on me just how the village has changed.

'Will you look at that!' he said. 'Eighty percent of the shops have got foreign names, some even in Arabic. Eighty percent.' He counted them. 'And there's even a mosque. In Pristina, a mosque for Christ's sake.'

I think he was more indignant because it sort of crept up on us all, but he came to it fresh and it was all there.

'The mosque's not really in town' I said, 'It's on their property. And that screen of hawthorn hides it off from the rest of town, really; we don't notice it.'

'Wasn't that part of the Weatherhead dairy, that lot?' Tim said. 'How did they get hold of any Weatherhead property? What have you been doing, Dad?'

So I had to explain to him about the bad year after the cannery closed down and the rust got in the wheat and the bloody bank said they'd foreclose. They don't understand these things, and they don't want to either, no use burdening them with your worries. So the long and short of it was I had to tell him about selling off nearly half the Weatherhead lands. They were in Mary's name but it's all the same in the end isn't it.

Oh, the Albanian cooperative I think it was called, it was all drawn up legal and it got me out of a hole I can tell you, don't you worry.

You would have thought I had sold the shirt off his own back, to hear him rant and rave. It was the first time I ever heard Tim show any interest in the land so it surprised me. No, it didn't but you know what I mean. Down deep we've all got a bit of the soil in the soul, don't you agree?

Still, it did take Tim's eyes to make me see what was happening and what had happened. He came in with the phone book one day, just before he left, and it was that little area directory, not the official one; the one that has all the phones and the businesses and the listings of all the little townships and villages over the valley. And there was Pristina: most of the names and businesses here are Albanian, he said. There's been an explosion.

Population explosion, certainly, I agreed. The Ibrahims set a trend, set an example for the lot of them, I've certainly noticed that, I said. They have fourteen kids – and a nicely behaved lot they are too, I said. But his brother-in-law – do you remember Belly Blaga? – Blaga has twenty one kids, what do you think of that? And the whole lot all living, the whole tribe of them. The youngest pair were born only last month, I said, and they're the third set of twins. Imagine that, three sets of twins in the one family. Belly Blaga, I tell you, must have the highest fertility rate in the valley. Though there are half a dozen others now bidding high to catch up with him. They really believe in large families. I used to think that was not only industrious, it was almost noble. Populate or perish, as we used to say. Now, well it's suddenly sort of overtaken us.

But their fourth girl, Melita, she used to help out when I tried the goat's milk cheese business that time your mother-in-law had all the allergies, thank goodness they cleared up though I don't know if the goat's milk did much help. Still, Blaga bought all the bits and pieces and the goats as well so I came out of it without much skin off my nose in the end. But you think of it, mate, twenty one kids. That'll make you glad you have only the two.

He didn't see the joke.

Before he left he made a point of going round to all the other families, even the Irish lot, though there's only a quarter of them left, if that.

Look, I said, if it's the mosque, or religion, or whatever, forget it. They keep to themselves, and there's even the Mormons at the other end of town, up on the hill.

When the Yanks came through with the McDonalds franchise and the Pizza Place, there were a few settled in this area, they were the ones to start the new fashion for toy farms and avocado or pecan nut plantations for their income tax. So check up on them Mormons, and the Christadelphians and the the Lutherans – lots of those further down the valley, I reminded him.

Tell the truth, I got a bit protective over our local lot. I still remembered Grandpa Weatherhead and his enormous pride in the way his workers scheme had paid off, and what he saw as their loyalty and gratitude.

Not much gratitude with the younger ones, Tim said to me. Damned sullen and surly, most of them. And of course I realised he must have felt himself treated as a stranger in his own home town. Expected to be recognised, even after all these years. Expected to be hailed and greeted and made much of. But we all nurture a little niggle in our hearts over those who flee the sinking ship. Those who are not prepared to stick it out. Nessie sided with him. And her mother, oh yes, Mary too.

And I've got to confess I am out of it all a bit myself, these days. I know my own crowd and having the shops keeps me up to date on some things.

But I was a bit taken aback when I heard the other week how the secondary school has just introduced a course on the Koran, and they even passed a majority resolution in the primary school against singing Christmas carols because it was cultural imperialism or something. That's going to extremes.

None of the ones I knew went as far as that. Though I do hear with the very young generation there is a growing fashion for the girls to keep their heads covered, even their faces and I did see a group of three schoolgirls, just last week, who looked more like an old Arabic photograph than anything I have ever seen right here in Pristina.

I think we have avoided some of the siller fashions, that is the good thing about a small country town. True, the boys in the garage down on the main road wore their hair long and ratty years after long hair went out of date, Tim tells me. And there was young Donnie Doolan who worked in the barber-shop for a while, he startled us all with his Mohawk. But that soon grew out and he was, you know, a bit of a pansy anyway so it was trying to upgrade his image, to use the modern jargon, and besides, Donnie's old man threw him out as soon as he shaved his head. I let him sleep in the room above the barber's for a while but it was clear he was a lost cause and I think we were all relieved when he cleared off. Kings Cross I suppose, somewhere like that. If you don't stick out like a sore thumb, in this town you get on all right I'm saying.

I don't know what will happen with this oriental fashion, but it really did get me a bit unnerved. Especially as old Mrs Gleeson told me just this morning that at the secondary school ninety percent of the girls are all registered as Albanian Muslims – even though the lot of them were born right here, in this country. Well, Mrs Gleeson says the pressure is really on among the peer groups for them all to go what she calls Fundamentalist. And Mrs O'Dwyer is sending her next girl over to Saddleback, to the nuns. It hurts, you know, hearing about that.

Nobody tells me anything these days, you know that. Part of the price you pay for being old, don't think I don't know that. And I would never have believed that selling the rest of the Weatherhead inheritance would have made such a difference in the way people treated you. Or, for that matter, how much that land meant in asserting the status of certain other newcomers in the place. Not that they haven't worked for it. But there's no attention paid, these days, to the pioneers and the people who did all the hard yakka of settling the district, making it what it is, giving it its name and its character. That's all gone.

No, is that so? A Law and Order squad? And who's behind all this? Wouldn't you know, but the pub's a good centre,

course it is. Bet they have suffered too at this upsurge of
religious puritanism among our Albanian friends. They
don't really believe in alcohol, in the Koran, isn't that the
case? Ernie's a bit of a hothead, always was. And what does
he think can be done about it? No, I hadn't heard that story,
sounds more like a mob of Irish ruffians, you ask me; more
like the days when those louts, all fresh back after the War
and trained in aggression, you remember them scaring the
living daylights out of Mrs O'Donnell down in the petrol
pump store, rationing was still on, you remember, and they
cleaned her out of all the fuel in the place when they hadn't
a ration ticket among the lot of them, caused her no end of
trouble later. But they settled down, all of them settled down
after a bit, needed a few girls to get hold of them, put them
in order.

Don't think this sounds like a case of a few sensible women
saying a few commonsense things, not with the way things
are, or the way things are going. I don't like the sound of it.
To confrontational by half.

Well, that's true of course, but in a sense we're all newcomers here, in the end. My grandfather might have called
this place Pristina and said it was pristine, but that's only the
half of it.

I bet you don't even know the old sacred burial ground,
down in our far paddock, the original one, way up by the big
cliff where the river cuts in, yes the Magic Mountain, that's
the one. We always knew it was secret, an Aboriginal burial
place. They would have been here centuries, thousands of
years perhaps. So if we are going to talk of ownership and
who was here first and all that, we'd better get things into
perspective if you know what I mean.

You go on, then. Leave me out. I was going to say that
of course I've seen it all developing and running away from
everybody, everybody that counts, that is. But I'm too old
anyway. This town isn't the town I grew up in, or the village

I knew as a kid. Of course I'd be sad to lose it all, but I will, you know, soon enough.

Just a minute. You've got to get this straight, it's the key to the matter.

All of those properties are paid for. Going price, hard cash most of them, not even on credit. Well yes, the prices were a bit low some of them, and I'm as much to blame for that – but you don't really think them being there devalued the land for others, surely you don't believe that, that's only pub talk, sour grapes. No, no no.

The Weatherhead land, yes I did sell that, and I did sell it to the Albanian Collective as I think it was called, I told you all that before. But it was the bank foreclosing, not the buyers that time, it was the bank. I had to sell for a quick realisation and anyone knows a man in that bind has to settle for the best that's on offer. A bargain then, well if you have to call it that. But I am not going to accept the blame for all that other talk about lowering values all through the district.

I'll give you that yes: population explosion. Who could have foreseen where that would lead? Do you think you could? They've always been polite to me and that's my last word on the matter.

No. No? Where was that? And who did you say was responsible? Gangs of them, that's a bit too much surely. Thirty seven, and Sergeant Miller confirms this? I'd put it down to the younger generation and not just the kids of one ethnic minority. Majority, then.

No, they've always spoken English to me. All of them. I think you're a bit paranoid, once you forbid a thing like teaching their own kids their own language, well you only make the forbidden more desirable. Young Ibrahim never spoke his language at home, never, he made a point of teaching his mother and she was the hard one but in the end she was trying to speak in her new language.

They do it to keep others out, to exclude them, you say?

Like a code? Look, they sit for their exams in English, they read the bus timetables in English, Gawd's sake, all the television is English, what do you mean?

Very well, I'll come over to the pub with you, right this minute. What do you mean, take the car? It's no distance, the walk will be good for you. Stared at? Ganged up on? Look, the pub might be the only building on the main street left with a local owner, as you call it (I still have reservations on the Irish) but isn't this a bit of a siege mentality? After all, they're neighbours, not enemies.

The Singer

Kester

You ask me about Juliet Klein? The town – our home town – was so proud of her, I was about to say the world was so proud of her, but you might just accuse me of exaggeration.

Still, Juliet Klein had a voice that almost defined its own era, just as, a bit later on, Joan Baez and Odetta defined the late 1960s or thereabouts.

Juliet would hate such a comparison. Hers was a voice for the 1950s, the decade that took to the long-playing record and stereo sound. There was a time when her 'Skye Boat Song' followed you everywhere, it was perhaps the first time music became ubiquitous, you couldn't escape it and you couldn't escape Juliet's almost painfully pure soprano. It was a voice that is now so embarrassingly dated. You probably know all that.

People said things about Juliet, but I loved her. I can say that now.

No, I don't know what happened to her, have you heard? You hear all those stories but none of them are true. Our involvement with each other was not in those very early days, out here, though of course we had known each other since childhood, how can you help it living in the same town?

No, I stood on the sidelines like everybody else, including her mum and dad and even her brothers Victor and Nelson. We all did, though, when Juliet made that extraordinary leap into international fame. I'd put it at three years? After that, well. Oh yes, there was the *Dead City* LP. *Die Tote Stadt*; it was a mistake, let us at least be charitable. Though the title song itself was haunting. It still haunts me in a way, in fact I would say I'm glad it did not take off like 'The Skye Boat Song', which I cannot bear to listen to now.

Not after all these years.

What seemed engagingly sweet and vulnerable then now appears quite phony, the singing teacher over her shoulder, that stagey little gulp after the first phrase, the one moment of vibrato near the end. No, it's funny how for years – four or five years at the least – that one song worked a sort of magic. And then, overnight, there was a change in the balance of the world and it was as distant and puzzling as Melba or Caruso on wax cylinders.

When Juliet and I had that extraordinary and tense relationship – it was extraordinary – she had been virtually forgotten as a singer for a decade at least. It was in 1972. London. Even that is probably before your time.

Of course you want to know the details, but let me put it into its proper perspective. 1972 was not the end. Not by a long shot. There was 1974 as well. Well, yes, 1974. The high and the low. The most and the least. I had never believed I would see myself grovel. I had never believed Juliet Klein would see me grovel.

Again, that's not true. 'See me grovel' – it's a phrase, I don't mean it literally. It's almost as if I end up saying the opposite of the truth each time. Gwen was brought into this – into this Thing with Juliet – perhaps if I were honest I would also say Gwen, or the absence of Gwen, while I was in London two years earlier was the very real trigger.

After all, it was because Gwen wanted me to contact Juliet in London – she had her address – that I made that fatal phone call. They were cousins you know, Gwen and Juliet. You haven't met Gwen yet, you say? In their early years Gwen and Juliet did have a sort of family resemblance – they were both very fine boned, fragile to look at but somehow columnar steel underneath. Gwen was a fine contralto herself, when she was young: in the Oratorio style, which is now so very outmoded. Her speaking voice had a similar tone to Juliet's, a slightly husky vibrato. It's interesting that Juliet had that soubrette sound when speaking but the instant she burst into song – she fluted into song, I should say – the voice always produced that quite pure timbre. I used to tease Juliet when she was humble enough to be teased. I called it her choirboy tone.

Look, let's forget the fifties. And the sixties for that matter. Gwen and I married, Juliet was in the States, I think, much of that time, I'm usually charitable and call it all the Revival Campfire decade as far as Juliet was concerned, anyway she made no more records, at least not commercially and I've only heard rumours of a cassette pirated from a live performance in one of those rusty church halls; Jacksonville was it?

Let me get to the point. My then wife Gwen was so loyal that when I got that International Travel Grant and it became clear that after three months in California I would be a month in London, it was Gwen who gave me Juliet's address and, more important, her phone number.

I had not even realised Juliet had been living somewhere in London. Telephonist for a taxi company, it turned out, not singing, of course, not singing.

I was in London nearly three weeks before I dredged up her address and phone number. You're right, simply to report back home at the end of the month, when Gwen and I reconnected.

How can I explain this with any effectiveness?

It was the voice, the timbre. It tore down fifteen years just like that. Juliet on the phone, that very first time.

It's the voice I'm talking about, not the body. The body had its own games in a way but that first phone call was voice, only the voice. Afterwards, when I walked away from that public phone in the pub on Bayswater Road and ordered a half pint, there was still that tingle, I could not concentrate. And I could not believe someone could take me over, quite against my will I can tell you. After all those years. Bloody Juliet. Bloody. Bloody.

Of course we had arranged to meet. That evening. You've unlocked me now, you've got to take the consequences. Juliet has moved in, as always, she has taken over.

Even here, even now, she has taken over. Don't grin like that, it only shows you cannot understand the meaning of it, the intensity of it. You think all things intense are only momentary?

Perhaps you are lucky. Perhaps you are not alive yet to the way things are, the way things might be. Some things continue, even underground, even unacknowledged, they continue. Like a curse. Like a sort of twisted blessing don't ask me to decide which, and does it matter? Like the vibrations of angels' wings. Juliet mattered.

I'll tell you that first meeting. That first re-meeting. Fifteen years ago? No, last week, last night.

I know everyone changes. And, remember, Juliet in those fifteen years had gone from being the soprano lead in the amateur stage musicals, into being an international star, an international voice rather. And then the voice blew itself out, the term these days is burn-out, but Juliet's voice was ice, not fire.

I know you don't remember, you're only a researcher you say, it's okay, people look blank these days when I say Harold Blair, or even Marjorie Lawrence. My growing up is full of voices that seemed everywhere, that seemed eternal, and which never bothered to have properly engineered recording sessions. You could say the same about Juliet Klein, except that last LP was all recording engineer sound, like a bathroom or like the early Elvis Presley echo chamber. *The Dead City*.

Juliet came up behind me on the concourse at Victoria station before I noticed her. She had been absolutely precise in her description of where we must meet and of course I respected that, it was a jolt back to old times in fact, a part of old times I had forgotten. Juliet and her precision. Juliet and her instructions. Juliet and her requirements that we all had to follow. In a sense we all went along with Juliet in that way. We all allowed her that sense of command, it was our connivance if you like, but it was genuine. We were all always so very well intentioned.

I was waiting, exactly as she had specified, with the light full on my face, looking outwards, near the main notice-board.

Even so, I was quite startled when she recognised me. 'And so, Kester,' she said, that voice almost at my ear, and her hand just brushing my shoulders as if to reassure herself I was still the same height. I was. 'And so, Kester, here you are, after all this time.'

You could say I gave a start. You could say I had completely forgotten her uncanny instinct for recognising people. In truth, though, I melted. My knees melted, even if I did not slump. I was instantly vulnerable. I did not turn round, Juliet was already fronting me, in her fawn gabardine, and we were embracing. Old friends. Very old friends. Old strangers.

It's silly. I thought of those old choir days, the rehearsals. The funny way we embraced, not to seem too passionate. Not to seem unpassionate. She was still the kid sister of my friend Victor.

Well, there was that time, the first weekend rehearsal for *The Merry Widow*, when we were all lolling around, lying on the floor, listening to our conductor's new LP of *South Pacific*, fifteen or twenty of us, a tangle of grubs on the carpet.

Juliet seemed to choose to lay her head with its long fair hair at an angle onto my tummy. Within ten minutes it was closer to my groin where her warm head was weighing against me. Then she did things with those blonde tresses. She knew what she was locating, though all the time she was making lazy comments to some of the other girls on the high points and the low points of the music.

Yes, a tease.

She had not changed.

We didn't even have to talk much. No asking about what happened when, who and where and the consequences. No talk of marriage – I still don't know if Juliet had ever married, though she soon enough had the whole case history on Gwen, but that's family, and when I married Gwen it was perhaps a subconscious marriage into Juliet's family as well, a step closer.

She could still have been sixteen years old.

Can you believe that? Sixteen years old going on thirty-something? I suppose it was the clarity of the skin. Juliet always had – so did Gwen – that golden-brown skin. Victor had it too. The gods, or the goddesses, know their aim when they fire. Juliet had her hair longer than I remembered, but we are speaking about 1972, mind, and 1957 was long before girls let their hair grow long and lissome and alluring.

All right, that's my generation, but it was the glory of those years, the freedom of long hair, girls swishing it around, flicking it off their face, letting it fall over their breasts, down their curve of spine as if pointing towards the firm curve of buttocks. Oh, all right, I'm only human, you've got to forgive me.

Juliet's first act, after that embrace, was to toss her hair back over her shoulder.

You're the generation that would probably say she was like Emma Kirkby, but I keep reminding you Juliet broke with the concert tradition. I tried to get her to perform, in some dim smoky pub that night, it was somewhere near the British Museum. Of course I gave up after a bit, though I can remember being tetchy, despite Juliet's long, still gaze that seemed to be directed back at me, and the way her hands had begun moving in that old, compulsive, blind person's fingering.

+++++

Juliet was quite happy to speak about her present employment. 'For the visually handicapped, it's a gift,' she said. Visually handicapped. That was her new term for it, in 1972. In her school days she wore those bottle-glass spectacles.

It was when she ceased wearing spectacles that I became aware of her translucent beauty. And she was always so damned independent. I admired her for that. Gwen always tried to smother Juliet, whenever she came up from Brisbane in those days, before we really became serious, Gwen and I. It was Gwen's nature, I'm not accusing her. That was in the days before Juliet had that little white cane. In London in 1972 the white cane was a compact, retractable model, high tech we would say now. Juliet used it surprisingly little.

When I took her back to Victoria and she instructed me to the right platform, I let her go through the tickets and onto the waiting train all by herself. I knew that.

'How do you know the train is in? Can you still see occasional glimpses?' I asked.

'It's the weight of it. There. I don't actually see it, I feel it. You see, Kester, it's not a matter of visualising, but of taking account of. Of weighting, if you like.'

Then she laughed lightly, and stroked my face, and left me.

Of course I waited. I watched, from the sidelines.

'Bitta orright, that wun,' said the ticket collector. 'I see her regular. Does shift work she says, keeps her outa peak hours. Got 'er 'ead screwed on real sharp, thet leddy.'

He gave me a wink. 'Carnt see a thing, y'know, mitey, carnt see a thing, just a sorta blurr she tells me, a sorta wash a light is what she tells me.'

We both looked at the train, now pulling out. 'I know,' I said. 'We've known each other since childhood.'

'Hey, I c'n pick thet accent, you're an Orstrylyun,' the ticket collector said.

'Too right,' I said, laying it on.

'But she's not an Ozzie, not her. Thet's not her accent.'

'Ah well, she was a celebrity performer. In her time. A singer. And singers, you know, have their voice trained, so it's different. But it's true, fair dinkum cobber.'

Was I going too far? I felt cocky and ebullient. It was Juliet doing it.

'I guess she was orlweys a stunner,' mused the ticket man, with that touch of regret in his voice. He was young, sturdy, rosy-cheeked himself.

'She was that, all right,' I said. I could not conceal the smugness, even as I continued with my put-on broad accent. 'The great thing is, she is still a stunner.'

That was the only time we really looked at each other, and he began to nod slowly.

'We all have our burdens, but some get them heavier than others', I said.

I knew it sounded pompous.

Silly, cheeky, confident, confiding, pompous: how could one person bring all these chameleon aspects of me out in such a harlequin muddle? I went back to my cheap hired lodgings.

There was an appointment the next morning but I cancelled it. First thing I phoned Juliet again and insisted on seeing her.

This time Juliet suggested I come over to her flat, she had two days off, and there was a little park nearby I might care to explore with her, it was her 'retreat'.

We had two days of passionate lovemaking.

It was the sense of physical touch. From the very first

moment of this second meeting, it was touch, touch, we could not get enough of physical contact with each other. We were voracious.

Later, that afternoon, after we had in fact strolled through the very ordered park with its over-green acid-bright grass and its as yet unmutilated elms (they would be all chopped out now, with the Dutch Elm Blight that was to follow) we ran – really ran – back to her flat.

There's no point in lingering over the details. I am assuming you must have experienced something intense and passionate and entirely sexual so you can substitute your own version of my specific giddiness.

Let me give you only one example. Large changes in our life can sometimes best be indicated by tiny details. And from that two day period of rapture and intensified awareness of everything I particularly recall the throaty low cooing of wood-doves, very early morning.

It was the park, outside, I suppose, the sanctuary. To wake with the air quite chilly outside the specific radius of our bodies, and to hear like a drone or musical burden the wood-doves repeating their hold on the world – I have only heard the sound a few times since, but it drives me almost to distraction with an old, unreturnable longing.

And, curiously, a sense of fulfilment.

Can I confide, even now – and to you! – it is a real sensation of union. We woke, on that now faroff morning, fully entwined. We had slept all night – or for some hours – physically joined, as if our innermost muscles would not let go after even the last hint of sensation. To wake – called by the wood-doves with their curious drone of insistence – and to discover that the dream of close union was no dream but the state of our bodies. Shared and sharing – you know, surely you know? – the true act of sex moves far beyond wakefulness, it is the point of intersection between wakefulness and the what we can only call dreaming, the body in flight, soaring. Angels with wings. So you can understand why I became, in a sense, imprisoned?

+++++

Look, I could go on. I did have to leave Juliet after those two days. Paris.

Paris? Well, another story, sharp, complex and limpid. I think I really loved it but the problem was I was seeing it with someone else's eyes, not my own.

No, don't be cynical. Juliet's eyes were impaired but that is not to say she was totally sightless. Her other senses provided a wealth of 'seeing' if you like. In my mind, I was the eyes, the observation, the explainer. Everything, everything I tell you, was as if through her eyes, and it was as if I were giving her sight to see and be part of it.

What happened?

Twenty four hours before I was due to return to London I was filled with this great sense of joy. I was not really in Paris in those last twenty four hours. Simple as that.

On the last morning I had a fight with the ticket officer in the Gare du Nord. It strained my resources and my language. And I battled through in trimph, simply because I became terribly aware that Juliet was the point at the end of my line of communication. I would not let anyone or anything – and a ticket collector in France is a formidable anything – get in the way of my return journey. I phoned the minute I reached London. She was quietly cold.

She had as it were thrown herself into the relationship but because it had a finite term she could allow herself an infinity of warmth and heat to pour into it. I can say that now.

At the time I was puzzled, then angry, then confused. I returned to Qantas.

Suddenly, it seemed all over.

Gwen

It doesn't need for me to say it. You've interviewed Kester, you know him I guess, from the horse's mouth. Or from the Ass's anus. Sorry. That was intended as a sort of joke.

Juliet is dead now anyway, am I right? Let's not dwell on what happened back then, the world has turned right over three times since 1972.

Besides, Kester romanticises things. You have got that much. I once thought that enthusiasm appealing. Now it is such a bore. Not that Kester and I exchange more than pleasantries at family birthdays.

Juliet did betray me. It took me a long time to forgive that, but I have, there's an end and we do not have to drag out skeletons.

Well no, it was not really England. When Kester returned to Australia I sensed right away there had been someone. I thought at the time it did him good. Eased him, as it were. He was more liveable-with. For a while.

I saw it as a bonus, and I did not have to ask who or where or when; England and travel is always a free time, a time out not counted in the real world or in the world of real relationships.

No. It was 1974. That is the hurtful year. That is the year Juliet betrayed me.

You did not know? But of course she returned to Australia in 1974. She was a guest of the Adelaide Festival that year. They were in their stage of reclaiming old local celebrities who had disappeaed into the distance abroad: Rolf Harris, Alan Seymour, Peter Porter, Lorna Sydney; they scoured the minor opera houses and the remainder bookshops for ancient Aussie exports. Not all returned, thank goodness. But Juliet Klein did, yes our Juliet did.

No, I don't know if her concert in the Adelaide Town Hall was a success, I arrived in Adelaide two days later, there was my Forum Club Conference and I was not going to miss that, and certainly not for cousin Juliet who had not bothered to write to me for over two years. I know why now but I did not know then.

And, let me be frank about it, my own singing career – I was a contralto – had been withered by childbearing and kitchen routine. At exactly the time Juliet was being famous. Of course I was jealous – though I couldn't admit it then!

Juliet's correspondence, at any time, was something like a postcard from Exotica written at her dictation by some Post Office clerk or gigilo or hotel menial. No, I am unjust to Juliet but who wouldn't be, no who wouldn't be, she was so damned, damned exasperating and so self-absorbed.

All those years during our adolesence when I carried for, when I cared for her, when I did everything for her – so that she could swan around as if everything she did was so easy and spontaneous and elegant. Why, she practiced for hours just to walk across the intersection as if she could see a thing.

I'm sorry, Denzel. Can you wipe that bit out? Just rewind and we'll go over it.

Juliet sang to a packed hall in Adelaide. Her voice was small but still pure. That's what the reviews said. You should check them out in, say, the Barr Smith Library. She did not sing the Skye Boat Song. In fact I'm told it was an almost insulting program, ending with Schoenberg's Book of the Hanging Gardens. Juliet always had an instinct for self-mutilation.

I came down on the Friday after, and when I arrived at the hotel I was shown the room Kester and I had booked. Kester of course came down earlier. The smell of Juliet was in that room. It was pervasive. I arrived at 11 am and they had not done up the room. The double bed was still a tangle of sheets.

Of course I recognised Juliet's smell. I even remember becoming first aware of it, it was strong but, well I can't explain. It was musky but somehow fragrant. I sound like a smell fetishist and perhaps I am. I was always scrupulous, myself, especially in those Queensland days. I was a compulsive bather.

There is a world of difference between imagining something and having to confront it.

What had happened in that hotel bedroom was irrefutably physical. And then the insult, later, of Kester trying to 'include me in'. I believe he was trying to suggest something like a threesome! As if he could please himself with both of us!

I cannot understand to this day how I remained calm and polite to the pair of them, how I even sat down with them to meals in the hotel dining room. We went as a threesome to two further concerts.

It was not until later. If you want to know I think it was twelve months, but I had a lot of thinking to do. And, thank God, I did my thinking. I worked out my own destiny and it did not include either Kester or – if you even thought it possible – Juliet Klein.

We were only cousins, though in a place like south-east Queensland we were family, of course I admit that. Perhaps in the end I only feel pity for her.

I don't have to feel anything for Kester. He scurried down to Melbourne. A good riddance. You say you have interviewed him already?

Yes, of course you did.

No, I don't know when Juliet died. Do you? You're a bit of a dark horse aren't you, Denzel?

I did receive a letter from some legal firm in Belfast, oh nearly a decade later, and it said Juliet Klein wanted me to have the enclosed pearl brooch, it was a family heirloom and they were acting on her instructions as per a codicil to her will made before her departure.

Yes, I thought that at the time, too. 'Departure'. On the other hand, I thought Belfast lawyers might be old fashioned and not want to call a death a death. Of course I heard nothing more.

It is all ended.

All of it.

Denzel

My mother is not dead. I could not say that to Gwen, though for her, let it be properly ended.

Sometimes I think my mother might as well be dead. She has given up talk just as she gave up sight. I think the giving up of sight was willed, by the way. It was a way of escaping.

Just as I was a sort of escape, but one that could not be disposed of easily. It is amusing, I suppose, that in the end she was a victim of her genes like everyone else, except that I was the consequence of her mid-thirties crisis and the desperation of the empty womb.

Didn't I fill it up! Didn't my old man, too.

To seek him out, though, all these years later: perhaps I am also a victim of genetic fixations and an incurable nostalgia. Daddy dear where are you?

And what did I expect?

I had a friend in Bristol who went on a daddy search and ended up claiming a manor and three well-paying tenant cottages that the tourists line up for in the spring and summer, Americans mostly.

My daddy was a – is a – minor radio personality in Melbourne. It is a regional Australian environment. I like that word, environment. I like my daddy too, as a matter of fact. Is that a disappointment?

I do not like my mummy, but whoever does? Tell the truth, it is the old dependency, I had to break free, I really did have to get away from the claw-like hand and the lovely oh so lovely voice always begging me just to help a little here or maneouvre this there, or that somewhere else, mainly friends or enemies but sometimes simply groceries or the light bulb.

I am cruel, I am ruthless. I have to be.

And her voice, it is a man-trap, all steel teeth. The strange thing is that my daddy, my new found daddy has actually convinced me (I think) that Juliet Klein in her prime was just the goods.

As a kid, I adored her.

The goods.

Just helping her I felt so important. Now, helping her, I feel used, a chattel, she hardly acknowledges my existence.

Do you know when it was in that first interview I realised my daddy was still hooked? Yes yes, he was still hooked and that made him more truly my daddy, poor idiot poor old lover-man, yes, that's my poor ol' daddy.

I brought along a CD. The Voice. And after he had finished slobbering and remembering and thanking me for showing an interest I gave it to him. I played it. It was put down only last year, a recording made in Brno, on a minute label trying to cash in on the capitalist market. The Voice Herself, yes you could tell who it was, though the range is now about two inches and the emotional depth just as narrow.

At least to me. But perhaps I am not exactly impartial.

I did hear her sing wonders, I think nobody else but I heard my mother try out everything from Paul Simon to Gorecki. I did even pride myself I was her best accompanist, but when the shutters fall from your eyes, well the shutters fall.

Her only late triumph was to catch onto this Eastern European pastiche stuff, you know, Schnittke and Pärt and Górecki, ecclesiastical imitations with a bit of folksy rhythm, a dab of Stravinsky and lots of monotony.

My mother was hypnotic at the monotony, endlessly repeated slow phrases, she wove them like a cat's-cradle, she used that narrow voice like a really profound incantation, she held a note forever and made you think it was the soul of music.

There I go again. She remains The Singer.

I nearly wept when my father grew so passionate, listening to that CD. Wept for him, not me, for music, for my mother too, yes, for my mother.

I did not tell him a thing. You learn tactics.

But of course I dreamed, again, the old impossible dream. You know, you must know. The one where my parents get together again.

Gwen, his ex-wife, like my own mother, she is implacable, she is unforgiving. I know her.

I wish to know my father.

All I know is that sons in the end confront and destroy their fathers, and hasn't he given me ammunition! I know I'll use it.

Still, that would be better than sons destroying their mothers and I think I have done that.

But then I think: without our life together, without me kicking out and kicking back and simply declaring that I am alive, I am me, I have to have my space too – without all those things, would my mother really have been able to add the quality of pain and purity and joy into her voice and that is what really gives her voice the magic depth in these new incantatory pieces that she has made her own. Even the composers of these pieces are almost servants to her voice. She has made them.

You see how it is? To have been made by her?

Kester, my father, is like me. He is on the edges of that. For the first time, with him, to be on the edge is to be somewhere. Fancy coming so far, so far back, to here, to her birthplace, to be somewhere.

I still cannot tell if Kester will be surprised. Or glad. Or desperate. What a bucket of guilt I'm about to unload all over him. What a little Game of Consequences. On the other hand, I sort of like him. I have all the cards.

Ljubljana

In the days when Slovenia had taken the first steps to independence from Yugoslavia by creating its own 'national
airline' – I am thinking of the late summer of 1989 – in those
times, if you walked through the markets or inner streets of
Ljubljana with its old Austrian colours and sturdy wooden
decorations, there was already a fine notation of difference.
'That man selling leather jackets, he is a Serb', my host
remarked to me. 'And that other one is an Albanian, the one
at the flowerstall'. To me, they all looked Balkan and my sight,
like my listening ear, was still far too superficial, stuffed with
novelty and a willingness to focus on the exotic. It was a place
that was consciously the most westernised of the Yugoslav
regions, Roman Catholic and scorning the cyrillic alphabet.
The famous Austrian composer Hugo Wolf was a Slovene.

But back then there was another frisson for those such
as me, visitors, people in transit who had no commitment
to anything other than curiosity or some inner catalogue
of contrasts – a sort of home movie mentality without the
cameras or the equipment. There was the still dangerous
thought that 'this is an iron curtain country'. Your passport
was evidence: what if you wanted to return to Australia via
America? By America, of course I mean the United States,
that segment of the American continent. Do not smile, I am
lifting you back to a time that was. To the time before. To
the Olden Days.

And in a very real sense, travelling to Ljubljana was like travelling into places where the darker fairy tales might well have been located. The clothes people wore: imagine seeing them in Melbourne? Oh yes, some of them would be wondrous in Sydney, at the right party. The Indian decade and the Greek decade had been and gone but there was still room for Central European chic, in fact it was only just beginning. I bought myself, from the Serb vendor, a leather jacket which I wore for several years in Sydney. It was styled with an aim for international consumers who might have broad shoulders and universal poppers. It could have hung in a stall in North Sydney.

When I was in Belgrade, the week before, I was told that city had been razed by invaders twenty-seven times. That was survival. It was also mutilation and revenge and a tenacious collective memory, armed to the teeth forever, unforgiving.

Ljubljana, for all its solidity and the provincial heaviness of its buildings, looked both venerable (to Australian eyes) and like some of those nineteenth century Australian towns planned in two or three storey brick on imperial models and believing they were facing the New Future, not the played-out past.

In the once-upon-a-time I was innocent, that is true. In Ljubljana I was open to everything. I was easy bait.

Andor was one of those people whose faces you forget easily, and then feel guilty. He had been scheduled to meet me when I flew in from Belgrade (on the Slovenian Airlines flight) and I have even forgotten how the connection was initially made. Was it the Embassy? Was it that helpful girl at the Airlines booking office? Was it a phone number someone had passed on to me, saying Andor spoke excellent English and his charming sister had once been to Adelaide with a group that had accompanied the famous (Serbian) poet Desanka Maksimovic to the Festival in, was it 1976? I had phoned him before making my bookings and he offered me everything. He would put himself out for me. He would be honoured. He would be proud to show me his city, his country, his people. I bought myself an extra reel of colour film.

It was the fag end of summer, really autumn but the weather was still and the sun seemed hot, it was as if everything – each leaf on each tree – was hanging motionless, stilled by the perfection of the season and the wish to hold on to it forever. It was the prelude to the Fall.

'My friend. You will see our town tomorrow, but I have taken the advantage of you and your arrival and I have arranged for you a special visit. Now. This very afternoon. Leave your baggage at your hotel, we are off this instant. I have a wonderful plan for you. You have arrived at the very moment. You must have planned it. It could not have happened otherwise. We have the special week of the mushrooms out in the country, it is our best kept secret. These mushrooms are magical. They grow only in one place and for one week only. I will provide for you a feast of our mushrooms, to translate their name you would say they are false toenails but perhaps I do not have the subtleties: fanciful delectables, perhaps, like little toes of young girls, very young girls with tender pale flesh you could take into your mouth and suck gently, each toe separately, till they squirm with delight.' His English was not perfect, but I laughed out loud at his jovial fantasy, and counted myself fortunate to arrive in the Week of the Mushrooms, no matter what they were called and in what language.

He had a small modern car and he drove fast. 'Slovenia is the industrial centre of Yugoslavia' he called out to me as we left the city outskirts behind. 'When we have our independence, we will take all the wealth with us. The rest of Yugoslavia is for peasants.'

We drove through green fields, clumps of woodland, and

increasingly into the area of rising mountains. The sky was almost cloudless, except for a tablecloth of white over the peaks that we approached.

Suddenly he stopped. We pulled into a dusty patch off the narrow road. 'Let me show you something' he said. He drew out a knife. It must have been affixed to his belt but I had not noticed anything under his convincing imitation of a Scottish tweed jacket.

'That looks sharp' I said, for politeness.

'Yes'.

He pulled out into the road again and we said nothing more about the weapon.

I did not see it again. It was not a portent – why should I think that?

'I will take you to one of our famous National Parks' he said, after some minutes of silence as we began climbing higher and higher. 'I will take you to Slap Savica, the water-fall that is the great source of the Sava river. You will have seen the Sava in full flood if you were in Belgrade. Did you see the Sava in Belgrade, where it joins the Danube?'

I nodded. Somehow, once having seen his knife, it had begun for no good reason to intrude itself into my thoughts. I tried to rationalise to myself that in these country areas, where antlers were displayed above portals and on condo-minium porches, there must be a long tradition of hunters and scoutsmen. I imagined wolves and bears in the over-hanging forests we had begun to have shouldering over the little car.

'Here. In this forest, they have released lynxes back into the wild', Andor said. 'They have gone back to their wild nature, after three generations, four generations in captivity.'

'Instinct must be very strong', I agreed, 'it must carry through generations' I said. 'And has the experiment been a success?'

'We wait. And we will see.' he said, 'But I have no doubts

about it myself. These forests have regenerated, after the war. Beech, Linden, Oak. Our wild creatures, also, they will revert to their real natures.'

We had moved, perhaps, into the cloud shadow by now. Despite the bright afternoon, there was a sense of darkness. Perhaps the increasingly steep cliffs that began to overhang the track had the effect of making everything seem more and more closed in. Darkness must be terrible here.

But we came to a clearing, eventually. Beyond was a flat lake, where the source of the Sava flowed in. It was a parkland, with rustic tables and benches. There were a few other cars and a group of white haired men and women were clambering down a precipitous track through the off-white rocks. They helped each other down.

'We will be the last visitors this afternoon. I timed it so. When we leave here we will head for the eating place and the mushrooms. We will arrive there just at dusk, and we will have our rare feast of baby-toe mushrooms.'

'That name, for an Australian, is pretty funny. I wonder what we would call these mushrooms if we had them growing in Australia?'

'You do not have these. Nobody has these. These are unique. Thus they are very special. As you will see. As you will taste. I promise you.'

His smile was contagious, even though its very crookedness gave his uneven teeth an extra prominence. But we have been pampered by the cosmetic uniformity of orthodontists and the like. In the context of Andor's well cut jacket and his neat white shirt with woollen tie, the quality of his smile enhanced the almost rustic fervour of his manner. I imagined woodcutters and forest dwellers as his particular ancestors. His Ljubljana sophistication – the excellent English, the very new car – only made this underlying rough-and-readyness more appealing. I was reminded, for an instant, of an uncle who lived at the Glasshouse Mountains. Not my uncle's unfortunate accident with the rifle, but something of his unpretentious grin, which my first wife found threatening but which was really only the fact, which he relished, of his uneven teeth. He called that smile 'his party trick'.

Andor held me back, until the elderly ones had fully descended and the narrow climb up into the rocks was clear. As we waited I gazed idly at the nearby wooden bench. Two upturned soft drink cans were littered there, and I mentally tut-tutted and thought how Western sins were seeping even into this place. Half a dozen European wasps buzzed in and out of the zip-openings. They seemed to be getting increasingly erratic in their activity, as if they were already drunk – at the aggressive stage. Andor caught my eye. 'Visitors! My niece, my beautiful niece, picked up one of these American cans and raised it to her face. She was bitten in the throat. Died. She died. She died in agony.'

I gasped and expressed condolences.

'It is nothing. That is life. But these American cans, they are to blame. They are natural temptations for the wasps and wasps do sting. Like the lynxes, they have their innate natures and nothing will alter that. It is the carelessness of man that I detest. Leaving these American cans like traps and of course the young children do not yet know, how can they know? My niece died in agony. She was very beautiful. I often had her at my place, I bathed her and put her to bed with songs and stories when her mother went off to … to her work engagements.'

'She must have been devastated.'

He looked at me. 'You will meet her. What she needs is a mate, someone to sire another child on her. Then she will forget Marissa.'

I understood there were complications. I thought I would welcome the extra company, though I hoped this awful incident would not be raised when we did meet. I was on holiday. Grieving parents were not on my agenda.

'Come,' And we set off on the hike among great pallid boulders.

It was a track that was more treacherous than I had expected. Seeing those aged people returning, all of them looking enthusiastic and only a little puffed, had tricked me. Perhaps they were all members of a hiking club and practiced their paces three times a week. Perhaps they made this trek to the source of the Sava three times every week. It was something about the place: obsessive, almost, and yet strangely peopled, populated with a sense of endless footsteps that had flattened out the path over the bruising stones, generations of pilgrims making their journey to this great Source, far back into pre-Christian times. It had the feel of a place of earth worship and dark primitive rites.

Andor was way ahead of me. Peremptorily he called me on. I was surprised at how easily I became puffed. I was not all that much out of condition, surely? He waited on a narrow wooden bridge over a small abyss and I could imagine him tapping his bony fingers against the handle of the knife, while he smiled me on.

'Past here. Around the corner, we come to the waterfall that is the source' he said triumphantly. I could already hear the noise of water belting down, and even caught a first glimpse then of misty spume, half way up the cliff-face. When I held my hand to the rough wooden rail of the bridge I could feel the vibration of it.

'This is a very old and sacred place. You must understand that. And you must throw into the water something of your own, something that has value for you. A coin perhaps.'

'But won't that cause litter? There must be generations of litter there, if that is the custom?'

'That is the custom, and who are we to deny these old rituals?' He said. But I sensed in his irony a greater reverence. I knew I would not dare to disobey his command.

I fumbled in my pocket.

'No. Wait,' and his hand again barred my own. 'You must see the waterfall that is the source,' he said, and the rhythms of his voice repeating the phrase again, sounded to me like some ancient invocation, or the start of some ancient invocation. I wondered how it sounded in his native tongue?

Holding my shoulder, he guided me along the track and around the last ledge and corner. The sight of the waterfall that was the source took my breath away.

It was much higher, larger, more imperious than I had imagined. When I had envisaged a spring emerging from the cliff, it had been a trickle, an almost mystical and precious symbolic flow such as I had once seen, in a remarkably vaginal orifice in the Olgas. This source was prodigious. If this was some ancient European manifestation of the Earth Mother, then it was like a monstrous eternal breaking of the placental waters, not a sexual flow of heightened voluptuousness.

The image that shot through my mind, in fact, was of a savage and primitive male power, the god pissing upon us and laughing; when the floods came, they would be calamitous. And that was the edict. It was a mixture of both male and female images, this place. Both of them bespoke power, not softness. Perhaps it was a merged sexuality I was metamorphosing at that instant: Whatever it was, there was something of ruthlessness in it.

'Throw your token. Now. Throw it'. It was a command. Some innate reluctance in me made me avoid reaching for the fob pocket where my coins were. Perhaps it was something in Andor, his peremptory tone, that made me instinctively seek out an alternative. I reached into my shirt pocket and tugged out a new ballpoint pen that had been given to me in Belgrade. I threw it as far as I could into the white water. It seemed hardly to reach the edges of the turmoil.

Andor looked at me sternly. 'That was not good' he said. 'You have discarded something. You must offer something you value. Money, that is always of value. Throw some money this time. Otherwise, you will be doomed to ill luck, to misfortune'. And he looked so serious I had to obey him, even though I tried to explain, in the car, later, that the gift ballpoint had indeed been special, and I had valued it. My offering of that gift was an offering of a special friendship, even though it had been one of those holiday things in a foreign city where two strangers became strangely intimate and sharing – bodies, language, these things do bind us.

'You were throwing away a little forgotten entertainment, then,' Andor said firmly. 'I think you were destroying evidence.'

I spluttered at that, but was not brave enough to deny it. Simply, it had seemed wonderfully symbolic at the time, in the moment. Money, money was nothing of value, why did he insist on that? He insisted on that.

Clambering back from the water, earlier, I was conscious of Andor hovering behind me. I think I would have preferred him striding ahead, like an impatient, eager gun-dog. There had been long slants of diagonal sunlight slashing through the tall slender trunks of trees, which struggled up as high as they could to reach the air at the top of the crevasse-like entry to the place of the source. Although he did not say it, I could almost hear him muttering behind me, like a chant, 'Soon be dark. Soon be dark. Soon be dark.' I had turned back to him, once, at a bend in the little track where there were fewer boulders, and had said, 'Surely it will soon be dark?'

He had not replied. The slanting blade of light had faded by then, and I noticed that his features were more swarthy than I had initially registered. It was as if he felt he had to urge me on, down that last slope. The waters of the lake, dark now as cellar floors, looked more turbulent.

Arrived at the car, he clambered in first. Previously he had always made much display of opening the passenger door for me. His first spoken words, then, had been, 'I am disappointed.' I understood how the sentence continued in his mind: 'in you'. I found myself growing defensive and spiky. I almost said out loud, 'Those mushrooms had better be good'.

But once the car was purring again, and we moved out into more open fields and meadows, with their soft green glow in the ebbing light, I persuaded myself that I had been rather imagining it all. It was as if the gothic atmosphere of the place, and all the intimations of old rituals and superstitions had overcoloured my too willing mind. Thank goodness there had been no overhanging castle in that cliffy gulley, with a portcullis and a miasma of carrion-eating birds. But it had been a place that brooded on its own isolation, I realised.

As if guessing my thoughts, Andor said, 'You should see, also, the castle at Lake Bled, and the island chapel in the lake, it is very famous, very beautiful. It is, as you say it, picture-postcard. Not like Slap Savica where it fills the waters of Lake Bohin.'

Out in these open fields, with the woodland retreating into dark shadows in almost orderly patterns, it was already growing hard to imagine ancient times of terrible splendour or those bloodthirsty battles so notorious in this part of the world. To Australian visitors, Bulgaria and Slovenia seem to inherit the same ghosts and folk tales. Vlad with his armies of impaled prisoners in serried rows; whole villages put to the scimitar in revenge for a single slight; populations razed and replaced. Old conflicts still seemed close to the surface here, I realised. And I made a mental resolve not to raise, even casually, any topic that might lead to an eruption of political claims or counter-claims. I had enjoyed Belgrade. Untactful to mention that now.

Finally Andor broke his sulks. He became the generous host again. 'This eating house we drive to,' he commenced, 'it is our best kept secret. It is naturally well known to the cognoscenti, but otherwise you are about to enter a purely Slovenian retreat of the senses: food as you will never have tasted it before; music, there will be music; servants in costumes of the area; and you will meet my sister, the one I have told you about, the one whose daughter, that beautiful child, is dead from the sting of a wasp in one of those American drink cans. But tonight you will share with me the delights of our own most intimate pleasures.' He laughed then, and it is true, I felt a ripple in my groin and allowed myself just a small and momentary indulgence, but put it aside as a fanciful response to an unintended double-entendre.

Language plays tricks with all of us, and when the language is not your own, it is so easy to commit even unpardonable errors. Only the week before, in that Belgrade hotel dining room, I had used a bit of my restaurant Italian to say 'Mezzo, mezzo' as the waiter too willingly filled my wide coffee cup. He had turned to me and whispered, in flawless English, 'Professor, you must be careful of your pronunciation, in my language you have just said to me 'shit, shit'.'

We suddenly turned into a small grassy lane, unmarked, untended. It was almost as if Andor himself nearly overshot the turn off. We bumped along this dim track for perhaps half a mile, then arrived within sight of a nest of lights. Their yellow warmth made me realise how completely the darkness had overtaken us in these last minutes. In the shadow of hedges and softly indistinct rolling hills, they looked welcoming and almost festive. The perfect hideaway.

As we drew up to the thatched portal, the heavy front door was opened and the sound of jolly dance music splashed around us, like the light from the elaborate candle-lit torch raised by the Majordomo (he couldn't be called anything less, I realised) as he moved out with a stately pace and a marvellous gold-buttoned uniform to usher us inside. This was hardly a farmhouse hideaway, I realised. It was the full opera.

We were ushered to a round wooden table at one side of the low ceilinged room, to a reserved table set for four places. It seemed crowded, but I was too fascinated by the whole scene to register with much attention the faces and attitudes of the others around us, engrossed in their own business. The room was large, that ceiling weighed down on us, but the decorations on the walls and several of the pillars that sustained the black wooden ceiling, were certainly artful. If I were cynical, I would call them the sort of imitation-rustic one might find in a Canada-Pacific hotel in Saskatchewan or Regina: farm implements, hoes, rakes, long scythes, fetishes made of straw, the usual worry beads made from garlic in strings, the tusks and antlers of long dead wild animals; taxidermised stoats, foxes, and in pride of place right above our table, a moth-eaten lynx. Andor explained to me that this was the last wild lynx shot in the area, and whoever was honoured with our table beneath its overview was indeed the night's special guest. No, he had not arranged this himself, he was a humble citizen in Ljubljana, he did not have such august connections. He congratulated me.

'What are the duties of a special guest, then?' I wondered. We were seated, but the others – his sister, no doubt, and her friend doubtless – had not yet turned up.

'Perhaps it will be surprise. Perhaps you will be offered the most choice mushrooms, the special ones,' Andor whispered across the woven linen. 'Perhaps the singers will ask you to name a special song.' His crooked teeth, in the candlelight gleamed almost green at that moment. 'Perhaps, who knows, my friend, you will be asked, as a visitor from a distant land, to perform something from your own culture. That would be a gesture, indeed, intended to honour a special guest. You see,' he added, 'in Slovenia we offer goodwill to our special visitors.'

This was the moment I had been dreading. Before leaving Australia I had been instructed by various knowledgeable friends that if I travelled to these distant places bound deeply into their own languages and their own cultures, I would have to be prepared to offer, at the right occasion, some 'Australian national song', some 'Australian national joke' or 'national recipe'. I had dutifully practised 'Waltzing Matilda' and 'Moreton Bay' (that was my trump card), and had even memorised a few drought jokes (water – or its absence – is always a matter of interest in countries subject to drought). I could, at a pinch, describe the gourmet delights of mud crab. But to date I had not been asked to put any of this patriotic duty to the test.

I looked around me. I realised just how inadequate had been my rehearsals and preparations, in the comfortable safety of my bedroom at home. I panicked at the thought of remembering all the words, all the stanzas. Or the punch line of the joke, which seemed suddenly to be either incomprehensible or impossible to translate. I assumed Andor had the verbal ability, but would he have the skills to evoke, in Slovenian, the nuances? Sweat began to break out on my brow, sticking my hair down. My armpits became suddenly clammy.

It was at this moment that I also started to realise that the rustic decorations were not all entirely guileless. Among the implements of the field were also implements clearly intended for other purposes: branding irons, a mace, several enormous swords and even what looked uncannily like leg-irons. And wasn't that, over in the far corner, an iron lady? On the personal rack of my own dread of public exposure, at some unnamed but inevitable moment, my imagination took unhappy flight. This was no mere farmhouse; it would have cellars, and they would be airless and the home of skeletons.

Andor was grinning still. 'As special guest, perhaps you will merely be asked to dance for us. In our country, we love the dancing.' He clapped his hands politely to the rhythm of the singers at the far end of the room. Their music had none of the complexities of folk music I had heard earlier, in wild but rigorous five-beat, seven-beat patterns. This music, I started to recognise, sounded much more simple minded, Tyrolean in fact, even to the incorporation of yodelling. But in four-four time, metric as a childhood beat, far too simple.

'This group, as it happens,' Andor pointed out to me, no doubt observing the way my focus had turned to the music, 'is from Austria. Our regular musicians are performing in Helsinki. They are famous internationally.'

There was no disappointment in his voice. He was enjoying this rustic music.

'Where are the others?' I asked finally, after we had been served huge plates of the tiny brown mushrooms, hundreds and hundreds of them, in their own sauce and without side-dishes or condiments. Thick wedges of heavy bread were the only accompaniment to the repast. Clearly, the mushrooms were to be relished for their own unique flavour.

'Look! What did I tell you? You have been favoured tonight.' Andor suddenly exclaimed with delight. 'For you, these are the most special of our baby-fingers.' And he pointed with his fork to a cluster of purply-brown mush-rooms at the apex of the great pile. I realised I would have to eat every single one of them.

'You will have wine yes?' Andor snapped his fingers. 'But for you, our honoured guest, the very best, the most special,' and he murmured to the host, that stocky old man who appeared immediately at Andor's beckoning.

'My good Australian friend, you are lucky,' he said with his solicitous gleam, a gleam I was beginning to have suspi-cions of, as I kept shovelling the pile of mushrooms. 'You will not appreciate your luck. Tonight is the night of broaching the new season's wine and as the first special guest on this special night, you have the great honour of tasting the first wine from the new cask. Of blessing it, in fact. There are only one hundred and fifty casks of this special chablis, it comes from the grapes of the Valley of the Martyrs, which we drove through as we came here.'

I knew I was being foolish, of inviting untoward, or politi-cally dangerous confidences. 'What martyrs were these?'

Andor chortled, a strangely boyish sound, more like a hoot than a chuckle. 'Ah, my friend, already I see you imagining the qualities of this special chablis to come from the buried remains of our celebrated martyrs. Alas, dear friend, a poetic thought, but not really practical. Those martyrs were four hundred years ago. We would have to fertilise the field with fresh crops of martyrs to maintain the quality of the crop, if that were so. Every year, a new crop of martyrs to be buried. I think our wine draws its flavour from less precious sources. You like the flavour? You must drink more of this.' He held his glass to the candlelight. 'We are most honoured.'

I think I had finished the full plate of mushrooms. I think I had drunk perhaps three capacious glasses of the white slightly fizzy wine. I think I might even have offered to sing a stanza of 'Moreton Bay' if the musicians would accompany me (I was sufficiently cunning to realise such a request was outside their repertoire). I believe I was mopping my lips with the thick, starchy serviette when Andor's sister suddenly appeared before us.

'You have neglected me. You have humiliated me. You have left me in Ljubljana without my car, and you have been entertaining our Australian guest all this time, you have been eating him up, you seek to destroy me.'

Her English accent was wonderful, full vowels, every consonant precise, each inflection accurate as a good recording. My first words, spoken with a rush of apology, sounded, even to me, broad and gratingly ocker.

'Forgive Andor. Please. He has been a beaut host and we have seen some pretty amazing places ...'

'So. And you are the distinguished professor, what is your name? Never mind, I am here now and you will make conversation while I catch up with you. Andor, you will order the baby-lip mushrooms for me immediately, it is the least you can do.'

Her brother was suddenly abject.

She was stunningly beautiful, and her name was Irene.

She smiled with a sudden change of facial expression as the formal introductions were completed. Her eyes were enormous, and made more so through obviously sophisticated use of subtle cosmetic enhancement. Her teeth were beautifully, wonderfully even, white and generous in her full-lipped mouth. They were, indeed, magnetic. I could not keep my eyes from them. Perhaps it was the contrast to her brother's unrepentant natural mouthful. Even her little pointy eye-teeth were still intact and, just like my daughter's, pushed slightly into prominence by the neighbouring incisors. My own dentist had, usefully, recommended that my Sarah's eye-teeth be extracted to allow the others that extra space. The result had been very successful. Irene might regret allowing her mouth to crowd out with everything that nature had provided. She smiled at me, and directed her attention fully in my direction.

'But what is this you have, professor? Surely this is not the first chablis of the season, and from the Martyr's vineyard? I see why you have both been sequestered without me, enjoying such a special privilege. You will not object if I take just a sip from your glass, Professor? Before my slothful brother thinks to order me my own serving?'

The act of savouring a wine can be a process of finest privilege. Irene knew all the subtleties and as she finished the rest of my glass her satisfaction was enormous, a reward in itself. She licked her lips, and then smiled to me again.

'You know the legend of this wine, my new friend? It is called the Eyes of the Martyrs. That is a beautiful name, is it not? The white chablis grapes it is made from, they are like beautiful eyeballs, and this wine is truly special. It is grown in the ancient Field of the Martyrs. They say it is because of their bones that this wine has its special magic. You find it a unique wine, surely? There is nothing like it in all of

Slovenia, all of Yugoslavia. You have drunk the eyes of the martyrs.'

Her brother did not correct her, or mention our earlier conversation. Irene had become the centre of a sort of whirlpool of activity by now, and everyone – the staff, the singers, even other patrons – seemed to be caught up in her dramatic and perhaps imperious performance. She may well have been an actor, and famous in this area: it was that sort of presence and projection.

Later events became blurred, no doubt it was the fresh wine which by this stage might well have been fermented from the eyeballs of ancient martyrs – or, as I seem to recall Andor maliciously whispering to me as an aside, from other sorts of martyr's balls, if it came to that. It is true, the evening seemed to be degenerating into something more ribald and full of secret winks, leers, whispers and suggestions. One of the Austrian Tyrolean dancers, I do recall, divested herself of her white blouse and I remarked, too appreciatively it seems in retrospect, at the wonderful milky whiteness of her breasts and the almost indecent pallor of her nipples. 'She must surely still be a virgin, to stay like that.' I think I even tittered. I know I imagined, at that moment, Irene with broad aureoles of almost chocolate brown and erect nipples strong as buttons. I do not think these thoughts were expressed in words at that stage. But they certainly floated in the air. I felt myself almost floating. I cannot even remember if the fourth member of our party turned up, though there is a blurred image of long tawny hair swirling, near my face. And those buoyant white breasts.

The darker fairy tales were certainly more and more in my thoughts, as the night wore on and the events of the afternoon blurred with the bubble of more wine glasses and the giddy effect, I was realising, of those magical mushrooms.

If I was a bear in the woods, and Irene was an all too

knowing Red Riding Hood or other pantomime princess, her brother was turning into all the other dark background figures of the scenario: the neglectful father, the sullen brother, the silent woodman, the vampire servant. And that shadowy later presence: another vampire agent?

Wait. Have I given too much away? Have I fancified it all just that much excessively? There had been talk of lynxes released into their old genetic hungers – or their feral futures. There had been, certainly, the waterfall and the source of the Sava, and striking enough it had been. More than striking, face up to it: it was damned nerve-wracking, a much more intimate and threatening sort of presence than Uluru or the Olgas. I was, myself, involved, not excluded.

And there had been the appearance of Irene, with her needle teeth that seemed to grow longer and longer as the night progressed. She ate her mushrooms with wolfish urgency, noisily, slurping and licking her lips. She even (I am sure I do remember this) lifted the plate at the end and licked it all over. She grinned then at me, as if to instruct me to do the same. Everyone was doing the same. The bare-breasted redhead was leaning over her plate to lap its last gravy.

The girl with the blouse; the girl without the blouse. If I think very carefully I am sure I recall, also, the host drawing down a long whip from the rafters and cracking it like a stockman to the rhythm of the accordionist. Did I try to explain stockwhip competitions then? And dare I remember that I did try to unleash the rain-after-drought 'national joke'? But by this stage there was a swirl of activity around me, and dancing, and the close proximity of bodies, many bodies. And animal cries, gruntings, farmyard laughter and smells and jostling activity, think of it all as a swirl, a vortex dragging the whole night into its centre.

I woke up. It was full morning. I was lying on an unmade bed and realised it was the hotel I had been booked into from

Belgrade. It had all the sensations that waking up alone in an hotel room instantly impose on us.

I remember what roused me was a sensation of strong itching. I woke up scratching my neck. As soon as I realised this I dragged my fingernails away. They were bloodmarked. I staggered then to the bathroom with its fussy Austrian sort of decor, and stared at my neck and throat.

There were several marks – four of them – and I had been scratching at these. I realised, immediately, that these must have been from bedbugs. I had once before, in Paris, experienced bedbugs and they made an unerring line for my neck and my throat. It must have been my own fingernails that had torn their little welts into lacerations, rather deep ones. And of course it was coincidence that determined these were spaced around my throat like two pairs of vampire incisors.

Bank Closure

Everyone saw it coming, but that did not lessen the small shock when the initial phone call came, followed by the formal letter with its proffered regrets and the terminology of rationalisation, which is another word for rationing. Rationing is something Bernard just remembered from the Second World War and after, when he was still a small kid. Rationing meant regulations and queues and going without. Sugar rationing was what he remembered, and the time he was almost scalped by his mother because of the experiment he and Beverley-over-the-road had been doing with homemade lollies. The lollies were a failure, the sugar was wasted – he still remembered his mother scraping crunchy remnants off the kitchen floor and swearing, actually swearing. Beverley was barred from the kitchen.

He had spent a great deal of his time rationing, if you think of it. Rationing, not rationalising. There was that period in secondary school when he undertook a long regime of rationing the aniseed balls. He cannot remember why, now, aniseed balls so obsessed him, but he collected them in their hundreds. He stored them under his bed in old Vegemite bottles. And he rationed them out to himself, one at a time, no more than three a day. There were only two of his friends who were ever allowed one aniseed ball from his store. They were Bill and Kenneth, and they swapped precious Malay States stamps for them. Even then Bernard was a sort of banker. When his father took him to the Commonwealth the first time, he was fascinated by the tellers, doling out coins and paper money.

Why aniseed balls? That's too far back even to worry himself with. It was a phase. Like the later decision to ration the number of times a year he allowed himself to go to the pictures. A year. Not a month or a week: even then he had a sense for the breath-span, as it were, of financial account-ability.

Later, it was not really surprising that he rationed the number of hours his own kids were allowed to watch TV. Even last year he had noted – or Jean had drawn it to his attention – that instinctively he had rationed the number of minutes he permitted himself to read the morning news-paper. She had timed him. At five past eight, after the ABC news, until fourteen minutes past eight. Bernard scanned the news like clockwork. Even if he had not reached past page three he would fold the paper (four squares) and give one of his little hrrrrmphs, and reach for the car keys. His official day had begun.

What on earth would he do once he had been forced into retirement? The prospect now stared him in the face and had done so since that friendly phone call. He had thought to avoid all the tension and pressure of competition and wran-gling for position when he had volunteered to manage the Cunningham branch. He had no ambitions for Head Office or even one of the larger centres. Cunningham was a small town but when he moved there it was one of the quiet little money earners. A number of small but profitable mines had their offices in the town, and there were the woollen mills and the butter factory, whose brand name was known throughout South East Queensland. The rich alluvial flats were first recognised by the explorer Logan, and most of the farmers in the district now had contracts with Heinz. A tidy little town, and the small but flourishing shopping centre reflected that. The year Bernard came in to manage the Commercial Bank of Australia, Cunningham was named Tidy Town of the Year.

After the Bank of New South Wales takeover Bernard retained his position, and his unwillingness to move was acknowledged. The branch maintained strong business, and because the CBA was in there first, it had local loyalties. Not even the Commonwealth had taken a foothold, and the Wales had always been only a sub agency. Well, that takeover was a 'rationalisation' if you like, but despite the name change all the old customers agreed it was only a surface thing. Old Fred Morrow had bought up six large chequebooks so that he could continue using the old bank name – Commercial, the proper name – in perpetuity. Or at least until he worked his way through them, which they both calculated would be four years. Good old Fred.

Bernard was one of the ones who had lobbied against the name change to Westpac. Perhaps that had been, secretly, when all the rot started and the inspectors grew less accommodating. But he had kept his ear to the ground and he was darned sure that Westpac would never stick. He lost the Ward account to the Commonwealth in the first month. Then all the Schinkler family accounts, the whole eighteen of them. In a small town, that hurts.

But nobody was to know the stranglehold of 'rationalisation', which had now come to mean, in the district, today, simply the drain to Head Office, down to the City. It had begun almost imperceptibly, perhaps because all the mines closed down one by one. Pit mining had become uneconomical and the State Government was giving concessions to open cut operations and their Japanese contracts. Then who would have believed the woollen mills would ever close? They had been exporting good quality stuff to markets around the world, it was boasted, though their domestic blanket brand was the stuff of their existence. Nobody foresaw the rise of the doona. Or the cutting of trade tariffs. That was the first nail in the coffin. Even the two real estate agents began to feel the pinch then.

A too depressing story. Bernard had survived it all, and some of the recent foreclosures had really distressed him. How could he face old Terry Maloney at the bowls club any more? He gave up competition bowling. He nearly gave up Rotary. When the Commonwealth closed down he did resign from the Business and Professionals. It had become a hollow farce, hardly enough for Whiteheads Cafe to bother with the catering. When Jean started to complain about the empty shopfronts he felt almost personally accused. He spent hours in his backyard vegetable patch. Getting his fingers into the soil soothed him, it had become his obsession. Though he rationed himself. After work, 5.30 to 6.30. Then he showered and was ready for the seven o'clock news which was always depressing.

Bernard was not, normally, a gloomy man. His long success in the bank had been, he was certain, because he had a deep cheery voice and he laughed a lot. He heard all the jokes circulating and delighted in passing them on as if he had just invented them himself. He had been often asked to give a speech at christenings and weddings and engagement parties because everyone knew he could keep them giggling and they would begin to relax. Secretly, he remembered some of those events and the long rows of weathered faces stuck with their own glooms, and sometimes it had been a bit of an effort, but when he did get them giggling and loosening up it was its own reward. He had felt his power and, being Bernard, he had rationed it wisely, not allowing himself to be carried away with his success.

He was known as a modest man, an ordinary bloke; but one who could tell a joke, even a clean one, and the women adored him.

It was not surprising, then, that he found himself out in the vegetable patch, the memory of the official notification still gripping his throat. He would tell his wife later. Jean didn't need to know just yet. She was talking about the trip to Port Douglas and somehow he didn't have the heart. Later, later.

As always, he slipped out of his suit and tugged on the old tweed trousers that hung on the back of the toolhouse door, with their braces and the leather belt (just to make sure). He buttoned up the flies. These old pants still had flies. He found the old shirt, one of half dozen or so he kept down there for the gardening, with its frayed collar and the missing button. He felt comfortable in these old duds and ready for the digging.

There were the potatoes that must be ready now. The soil down that end was clayey and had taken a lot of breaking up with fresh compost and some fertiliser; the spuds should be whoppers, he estimated. Two weeks ago he had made a tentative dig and resisted the temptation. Patience was always one of his virtues. Now it would be rewarded. He measured out the broadest spade, the one that his father had given him, back in the early days. The old man had been a tyrant, but it was amazing the number of things Bernard still retained from then, and the number of actions and habits that endured. Even the gardening. As a kid he had rebelled – or he imagined he had rebelled, though it was simply a matter of demanding some time for himself on a Saturday morning. When he did force his father to give him time off (one weekend in four) he found himself bored and with nothing to do. Even his stamp collection seemed hollow and worthless. It was an evening thing, it did not feel right to be a Saturday Morning pastime. He had returned, of his own accord, to assisting his father, who then gave him his own bed to look after. He still remembered the pure joy when he dug up his first Bernard potatoes, as the old man called them. They made a ceremony that very night, a special Bernard potato dish, with butter and a topping of cheese. It had set him on his way.

Still smiling to himself, remembering all that, Bernard ambled down to the back bed. Was he humming just then? He turned the first sod. Yes, the soil was still pretty raw clay, but not as bad as when he first turned it over and of course he should have put in more compost but it was a start. It was a shale mixed in with the clay down this end. That made it harder and was probably why he never bothered to prepare this corner of the allotment for veggies until now. It had remained grass.

Shale was still mixed in with the clay and the compost, and the first potatoes he uncovered seemed to nestle under and around those lumps of pure rock, or perhaps even to split them up with their subterranean energies and movement. Perhaps a couple of seasons with spuds and they would do the work of their own accord, saving him effort with the pick and mattock like this time last year when he first began the bed's preparations. A bed had to be dug, and aired, and composted, and then dug again, and given time to settle, his father had always said. Bernard had rationed his activities and the result was now paying off. The first spuds are generous, more than he hoped for, if he is honest. They will keep, though; they are not the starchy variety that rots easily.

Digging for half an hour, almost ready to call it a day (he looks at his watch: 6.15, give it another ten), Bernard rests on the shovel and wipes the sweat off his brow and the top of his head. It is bald now and his weekly barber visit has become a farce, but old Ernie needs the business. It is one of the little duties that stuck. It is an old habit. Gazing idly down he can see a potato he has missed, among the upturned rubble and shards. He bends down.

Stuck to the tuber with clay there is a rather large, flat stone. With clay sticky hands Bernard wrenches it off and is about to toss it over to the fence, where he has thrown several other larger stones. Something catches his eye. He looks closer. The potato had split the shale – two pieces fall neatly apart in his hand. He rubs his eyes. He wipes one hand on the old trousers and pulls out his spectacles from the buttoned-up shirt pocket (Too many times he has had to slouch back to the shed for them. He knows how to rationalise his movements, a real time and motion expert). Putting them on his nose he looks closer.

It is a fossil. A fossilised sprig of leaves. Not a fern, something larger than that. More like the leaves of the Queensland kauri pine in the Municipal Gardens. A multipennate sprig, he thinks, remembering from somewhere. Seven, no eight, leaves neatly branching out from a single stem. They are remarkably lifelike, almost as if they had not been underground long enough to rot or decay. And that is the point: the slow process of earth, of weight and heat and enclosure have taken this one twig of an ancient tree and pressed it to its heart. It has been immortalised. Fossilised.

Bernard stares at it for a long time. Something as ephemeral as a single twig of a tree, no doubt one of thousands of trees that had grown and lived here sometime, something that had seemed ordinary and simply part of the busy or lazy life of the valley, Now it was singled out. Now it was made special. All of the endless days, one like another, and he was able to see them as a preparation for this, this accidental uncovering, this discovery. And he had made it. It was his. Discovery is not the new, or the novel – it is the recognition.

It was not easy to describe what he had found, even to himself. Bernard's jokes had not prepared him. He found himself trying to uncover fossil jokes; he was already thinking of how he might try it out with Jean first, and then even make it part of his line with the customers, who must be told of the information in that letter and the closure of the bank and the end of the eighty-five years of continual commerce that it represented. He must indeed think of how to break the news lightly, how to ease the pain.

The potato had broken the slab of shale lightly, to uncover

the fossil. It was not Bernard, it was part of the underground life of the spud. The fossil was part of the underground life of the soil, that was more like it. The whole place was full of forgotten or hidden histories, none of it was virgin soil, none of it was meaningless. Grinning to himself now, Bernard moved automatically up to the house, ten minutes early, and with his working boots still on. He tramped into the kitchen as he was, without the surface washing that always preceded the shower. He stomped over the floral carpet of the living room. His wife was setting the table. They always ate at the main table even though the kids have long left them. It was one of their routines.

'I found this,' he announces, but Jean sees only an ochre-coloured slip of rock. When he points out the fossil and the seven – no eight – leaves with the stem almost as precise in its fibres and veins as a living twig, she is about to say 'Really' and then chide him. But something about his look, almost boyish and wide-eyed, makes Jean remember, quite suddenly, the young man she had first courted and who had to be nudged into marriage. Those had been exhilarating days and she had felt the first surge of fulfilment.

'Should you advise somebody? The Museum perhaps?' she says, instead. And they both grow rather excited, as if they had unearthed some real treasure. Almost as if they had unearthed a mastodon tooth or the shoulder of a pterodactyl.

Later, Bernard looked up the *World Book Encyclopaedia* that had not been touched since the kids, and could find nothing that might classify their fossil. It was a tree, they decided, not a shrub or a grass or a creeper. But that was only because it reminded him so much of the kauri leaves. That night he stayed up unusually late and they talked about the news which had broken upon him earlier. He finally was able to broach that with his wife.

He had not mentioned the telephone call two days before. He had lived with that contained in his procedures and his habits. He had rationed himself carefully. It had remained inside. It had fermented.

When it did come out, finally, in the long talk around the table as the gravy grew cold and the steak bones were declaring themselves and the slivers of fat were congealing on the sides of their plates, Bernard was quite open; he almost made it a joke, though he did not call himself an old fossil and he did not actually utter the word 'retirement'. Jean realised that Port Douglas was out of the question. She had always felt they were living on credit.

But it was possible to discuss their future. That was like a burden lifted, like a long weight of clay that over the past two days had weighed down this news upon him. He did not speak of himself at all, really; he spoke about the town and the economic effects of the bank's closure. He joked that the only person to benefit would be the Shell service station. Everyone would have to drive into Somerset to do their banking. And their shopping. Fuel usage would increase. 'That's if anyone can afford to pay for their petrol,' he added, and they both laughed as if that were a joke. Shut-down. Closure. Even as they discussed it they could not believe it.

'What will happen to the records?' Jean asked.

'They will go into archives,' Bernard answered, but that did not encompass the history of the whole town as expressed in those figures, lists and records. It would be submerged and forgotten.

The fossil had been washed of its clay, very carefully. It sat on one of the Noritake platters for most of the meal, and after the long talk and the almost delighted realisation that they had missed the TV news and the *7.30 Report* as well as *Quantum*, Bernard had picked it up yet again. Why did he feel so elated? Why did a commonplace thing like an unearthed fossil – in a district well known for its fossil potential, hadn't the University sent students here for decades? – why did it leave him feeling – what?

Positive, was the only word that came to him, but it was other than that, more than that. He could not explain it, even to himself, but it made him feel curiously connected.

'Now I know what a scientist feels,' he quipped to his wife, as he did the drying up. 'Or an explorer. Or a discoverer. Silly, isn't it? But I will take you up, dear, and phone the Museum tomorrow. Though it is probably nothing valuable.'

'It's valuable to you, though. To us.' And Jean passed him the Noritake platter, which he handled carefully, though his thoughts were elsewhere.

The person at the museum was cautious but just a little responsive. Could he bring it in for identification? Was he ever in Brisbane? Very well, the week after next, then.

Bernard was just a little regretful when the Museum took it from him. 'You've heard of the Wollemi pine? The one they discovered in Wollemi National Park a few years back, that they thought extinct for millennia? Related to the bunya and the hoop pine and the kauri. It was known only from fossils. Well, I'm not saying this is a fossil of a Wollemi pine but we'd like to do tests. Tell you the truth, Bernard (why were these public servant types always so familiar?) I'm just a little bit excited myself. It must be exciting for you, too, if you have uncovered something really interesting?'

But the excitement had been subsumed by the ordinary events of living and confronting his future and his customers who had all been sympathetic though quietly angry. Bernard had forgotten the moment of discovery and that long animated conversation at the dining room table, when he and Jean had been close in a way that both seemed almost to have forgotten.

He had even forgotten to gather up the freshly harvested potatoes until the next evening. They had enjoyed them, though, and they were not really surprised that Bernard poked further, but had turned up no new fossils.

The Museum never returned the treasure, and, indeed, Bernard never discovered what they finally made of it. When his garden bed had been dug up and thoroughly prepared a second time, Bernard planned to grow legumes. Then, the following year, it would again be potatoes.

The day that the bank closed its doors, finally, he decided to make it a picnic, under the Kauri pine in the Town Gardens. Bernard's potato salad would be remembered. Nobody had turned up yet from Head Office to look after the official bank archives, which Bernard had labelled, tabulated and prepared according to a system that had already been forgotten in the big offices in the city.

But at the last minute Bernard knew he had a final duty to his customers. All his scrupulous personal notes and annotations on every bank client over his entire career at this branch – a veritable history of the town – had been kept in the red filing cabinet in his office. How could he allow all that to be consigned to some dusty vault or even a shredding machine in an anonymous basement?

Bernard carefully conveyed his alphabetical files to the little back sewing room which he now made into an office in his own home. For the first month after the bank premises had been locked and the building stood empty and dusty Bernard went through all these files and memos, discarding a few, reorganising others. He would dress in his suit and business tie each morning and even, for a little while, made his ritual local visits – the weekly barber, the newsagent, morning coffee every second day in Whiteheads Cafe with the postmaster and the solicitor and the local police inspector. But his records claimed him, finally.

Much later, after he had done everything possible to tabulate and finalise all his records, he was watching *The Gardening Show* with his wife one evening and was intrigued by a demonstration of composting that used wads of old papers. They disintegrated with surprising speed under a mulch or a load of good heavy earth. The demonstration featured how a clay patch had been rendered malleable and suitable for roses.

The next morning Bernard went out early, in his old gardening clothes so that even his wife was surprised. He spent an hour digging and preparing. Then he went to the little sewing room and came out with the first of the dun-coloured manilla folders. Carefully he layered them, one by one, in alphabetical order. Then he applied the half broken-up clods of clay interspersed with some rough sand from the ancient children's playpit. He covered it all with what he could find of mulch from the compost heap. He rubbed his hands together and went indoors.

The next morning again he dressed in his gardening shirt and the old saggy tweeds. Without thinking of the effect he wandered down at 10.15 to the cafe.

It was the day for morning tea.

Furry Animals

Pity is the most dangerous of passions. Sympathy is almost as bad. You think you are strong, in control, and generous when you pity someone or something. You are at your most vulnerable.

Take yesterday. The heart can be sickened, I tell you. It's like indecent exposure – it's not the visual demonstration of miscellaneous body parts, but the willingness of it all. It repels. Similarly, yesterday's display made me cringe. It was outside Flinders Street Station, on those steps where hardened druggies lounge and have commerce with teenage rebels who pretend that black leather and lots of decorative chains make them, too, hardened. You know the scene.

Yesterday midday. Shopping crowds, lunchtime crowds. The regulars had taken their positions and so hardly moved to let the ordinaries pass through. The vendor of newspapers and plastic-covered girlie magazines was taking the sun while it was there. Two policepersons strolled through like familiars, checking out or lining up or seeing who's new. Every now and then a dusty, gusty wind wiped its sleeve across people's eyes to make them sting with the grittiness of the place.

And the trams continued to rattle jerkily by, clumps of them like goats stopping for water, and then long periods when not a one jostled into view.

Weekday ordinary. It's precisely that sort of time when you start to shove your elbows out and your briefcase in the battering-ram position. And yesterday morning had been more than usually fraught. Moira had phoned. Worse; she had threatened to come in. So of course it was inevitable that I decided it was necessary to take the train out to Hawthorn for that audit job I had been putting off. The train, because I could check through the files on the way. Trains are always more relaxing. Relaxation is important. Relaxation, in my job, is essential. Moira is not good for personal relaxation. Moira is not good for anything, except reminding me of the children's expenses. Don't get me wrong, I love my children. But to have an ex-wife who was my senior in the other accountancy practice is not inducive of relaxation. She even adds-in postage stamps and itemised lolly-wrappers when she presents her monthly Statement of The Children's Expenses. She is a lolly-wrapper person herself and I know the dental bills, in due course, will be higher than the laundry lists. On the weekends when I have access I empty out their pockets and their backpacks on arrival (though I return the confiscated confectionary on departure. I am scrupulous in this as in other things.). As I cleared a space outside Young and Jacksons, waiting for the green light, I tried to put Moira out of mind, and to focus on the last Hawthorn audit when, as I recall, there was a matter of a ninety cent shortfall in the Petty Cash register.

I allowed myself to become engrossed in the problem, even though I knew that as soon as I got into the carriage I could verify from my notes (was it ninety cents or ninety-five cents?). I almost missed the green light.

It was in that sort of slightly inconvenient but sufficiently distracting lunchtime buzz of activity that I knew thoughts of Moira might happily be replaced by more realistic priorities: such as, would I have to wait more than ten minutes for the Belgrave or Lilydale train? And, if so, would I cost-in that travelling time onto the client cards? Or would I be generous, and take out my raisin-and-vegemite sandwich, in which case it would be not travelling time but lunchtime?

It was in the midst of such a fine nuance of considerations, on the very steps of Flinders Street Station, that the giant furry koalas appeared.

Big, person-size koalas. Koalas of the appropriate grey colour with big white ears and carrying plastic buckets which they rattled.

I guessed these grey koalas were Greens.

I was not close enough to see if they had banners, or leaflets to distribute, or even if they had SAVE THE WILDERNESS stencilled on their koala chests. I suspect they did not carry in their pouches receipt books with the appropriate authorisations allowing donations of over $2 as concessional deductions under the Income Tax Assessment Act 1936 As Amended. I also suspect they were not GST Exempt.

None of this, it seems, had daunted them. They were not timid little pets or Protected Species at that particular moment. They were soliciting in public.

That, really, was when I realised that we are victims of our juices of pity, captive to our own sympathetic drives. We fashion our own passion into unguarded vulnerability. I was glad I did not have Amelia and Louise with me. It is not good to see your own father wanting to run away from such a koala onslaught.

Those yellow plastic buckets were weighing the koalas down with gifts. Maintaining with dignity a deliberate pace I did notice that not even the two policepersons had queried the operations of those creatures.

More. Those two furry creatures stood in front of the most hardened toughs, not speaking, not waving, and I actually witnessed how those defensively snarling faces broke into soft lines around the mouth and eyes and an altogether different cast of jaw. Grandmothers would have said, 'I knew there was some good in Ted or Tess,' and fathers would have wiped a brawny forearm across their eyes to stop the tear dropping into their beer. They would have mumbled, 'Course

I kicked 'em out, they was getting out of hand. Shoulda seen 'em when they was kids but. Jeez, shoulda seen 'em.' Fathers, mothers also, walking towards the January sales in Myers shoved into purse or pocket for a coin when the Giant Cuddly Bears stepped in front of them. I was right to feel under pressure. Thank God the children were not with me, I would have committed unpardonable acts of generosity. As it was, I even saw one of the policepersons throw a $2 coin. It was with some relief that I noticed the other policeperson look the other way. Vulnerability takes all of us at unexpected moments.

It was clear that the second policeperson had been caught by furry creatures once too often. That one had no time for pity. But I caught myself imagining (as I saw her standing arms akimbo while she waited for her gullible male partner) that she was speculating whether the furry bear whose yellow bucket was still thrust forward invitingly would be male or female. She was a clearly an officer of the law after my own heart. A sort of Honorary Auditor. I imagined her demanding a public unzip.

No, nothing like that happened. I am, after all, a responsible citizen. Any public exposure is, after all, indecent. As it was, I was feeling particularly exposed. I hoped that nobody had recognised me, though one of the advantages of using public transport for small audit jobs is that measure of anonymity. Nobody suspects you. And you often hear the most revealing conversations. I have a friend in the Tax Audit Branch who enjoys my confidences. The furry bears went on their way towards the Saved Forest. The skinheads wiped the sweat off their shorn features and remembered what they were here for. The newspaper vendor remained inviolate. The two policepersons plied their trade. Another tram came into sight up near the War Memorial.

Yes, pity makes you vulnerable. You open up and you open out. You give, when you damn well know this is the Year of

Take. You want to be generous, when the decorums of Meeja Greed know better than you what you need.

The newspaper vendor is not bluffed. The newspaper vendor has the strength of an ikon. The newspaper vendor is as cynical as a journalist.

It is only people like us, in the middle to lower ranks of the social pecking order (as Moira was always telling me, from her superior perch two rungs up the ladder) who are part of the furry koala give and take.

Or who might be in danger of being.

Perhaps those koalas were not really cadging for Rainforest Preservation, Endangered Animals, or what's left of the Right Whale. Perhaps they were part of a campaign for a new line in Koala-skin Muffs or Emu Pies or the South Australian invasion of Kangaroo Chops?

I know that I'm making this up now. I'm aware I'm being over-defensive. I can see how others side with them, the Big Koalas. Of course I can. I know I'm outnumbered and out-voted. And of course I realise that auditors themselves are a despised species. Oh, Moira was right when she told me 'Move into financial management. That's where the future is.' As well she proved. And yet, I have to confess it, there is something about the work of an auditor that I enjoy. I feel truly at home sniffing for errors and snouting out the little tricks and deceits of the junior clerks. Big corporate frauds, of course, are beyond me, I refer them to Upstairs. But give me a day with stocktaking registers, or – as in the Hawthorn case – weighing up flour delivery quantities with production output of bread, cakes and confections, and a calculator can uncover wonderful discrepancies. I am in my element.

What really infuriated me about those canvassing koalas at the station yesterday was I, too, almost weakened. My fingers almost went straight to the coin pocket. It was only that ridiculous policeman saved me, in the end. The moment I saw him fumble, and throw his $2 coin, I was filled with contempt. I felt for my green pen, instead, and repositioned it in my shirt pocket, next to my heart.

Don't get me wrong. I do keep receipts for Tax Deductible Gifts Over $2. I have supported charities. Look, I am a simple auditor. I do not have a plastic-coated identification card proclaiming me a Tax Inspector (though sometimes I have aspirations). I have learned to live with myself. And with the two girls on alternate weekends. I have taught them chess and Scrabble. I live a very ordinary life, not like Moira with her Opening Nights and her Musica Viva. I am a very contented person. Auditors know the satisfaction of a job well done. I'm not a member of the Mafia intent on elbowing into the act. I have no subscription to the Loggers Association or the Pulp Mill Manufacturers Monopoly. Look, I even like cuddly, furry koala bears.

That, of course, is the trouble. Koala bears are not cuddly and furry, they have very sharp claws and if cornered they come out fighting like any one of us godless bastards. Koala bears are immune to pity. How could anyone believe they fall for sympathy? I would put it that they keep to themselves and are territorial. Have you ever seen a real koala bear traipsing round with a plastic bucket asking for handouts? I rest my case. The moment you give way to pity, you're undone.

But what really gets me is the way those skinheads and young thugs began talking to each other and even some of the old mums on the steps, right after. It was as if they thought they were onto something. Generosity, perhaps? A Good Cause?

They wouldn't even know what a rainforest is. On the corner of Flinders and Swanston streets there's not a single eucalypt in sight.

If I had not been forced to fumble for change at the ticket office I would have seen none of this. This aftershock. But, having seen, I carried it like a file of unexamined documents in a manilla folder, onto the platform, where I did have to

wait all of ten minutes, and in all that time, when I could
have been going through the Hawthorn file in preparation, or when I could even have re-examined Moira's earlier
documentation of the children's costs just in case there was
a mathematical error or some dubious inventory item that
could have been classified as partly her own (I am ever the
optimist), no. I found myself thinking, still, of those lum-
bering koalas. It was as if they roused some hidden response
mechanism in me, as if they were making a claim deeper than
that even of the children (who rejected teddy bears in favour
of Barbie dolls years back). It was that hidden claim which
was the real hurt, the potential exposure. Pity is the most
dangerous of passions. Self-pity is unforgiveable. I found
myself writhing on that station platform. And for no reason
that I could clearly allocate.

It was only as the train was pulling into the Hawthorn
platform, with its 1890s fashionableness come full circle, that
I realised where and why the koalas had inspired me with
such instinctive love and anger. Yes, love. Fortunately, anger
is more permanent.

My brother, Bellamey, would have called my initial reac-
tion pure cupidity. He was always defending his teddy bear
from my clutches. That was his way of saying it. But I loved
his teddy bear with pure ardour. It wasn't avarice, not at all.
It had purity. And when I did take the scissors that time and
then carefully unstitched every seam (it is a moment I recall
with great clarity and satisfaction) I think it was a sort of
delight, as well as the dismay I so loudly voiced, that brought
our mother running. There I was, tossing the stuffing all
over Bellamey's bed and his teddy bear was truly dissected.
That was the incipient auditor in me, even then.

It was because I had no teddy bear at all. Not one. I had
been given a gollywog, despicable creature. Bellamey's teddy
bear was my first true love. Love, as we all know, does not
bear analysis. After, I swore I would never be vulnerable

again. But we are taken by surprise each time. When I told Moira the story of the giant koalas yesterday afternoon, in Laurents where we usually have our Progress Reports and Interim Settlements (by which time I had it already polished) I intended it as a sort of shield against further demands. But Bellamey's bear slipped into the conversation. I was deeply surprised when she leaned over and gave me a peck on the cheek. It was the first time in two years. That was when I fully realised that pity is the most dangerous of passions. I felt as vulnerable as some junior clerk when the auditor's arrival is announced. I could not afford to let Moira know this. When she settled down again I said to her, I hope lightly: 'Well, what would you have done in my position?'

'I would have saved up and bought my own teddy bear,' she said instantly. 'Oh, you mean about the Flinders Street money-bears? Arthur, I think I could have easily offered them a ten dollar note.'

I was shocked.

I didn't say it, but I thought: 'That's my money!' I had just given her the cheque for the children's allowance. And yet, in my heart, I knew how we differed so utterly. She would have bought her own teddy bear. There was only one teddy bear in the world. And it was Bellamey's.

Sunshine Beach

One

You don't have to take it lying down, he thought to himself. Where is that bit of canniness you prided yourself on, and your wife derided? Old moneybags, old stick-in-the-mud, old party-pooper. He had forgotten how reassuring and lively their backchat had been, how it kept him on his toes – of course he knew it did. Not that it made some of the gibes easier, but he had had his own defences. Or, as Miriam would have said, his own fences.

He had always said to Miriam that it would be him, Charlie, who popped off first. Miriam, with her angina problems and the long business with the osteo, was nevertheless strong as an ox; she had her mother's genes and old Hannah was still bridge champion at ninety-one. Miriam was the sort of person who walked into a room and was instantly at the centre. Charlie had become a sort of shadow, there to make sure or to divert the more obvious bores and the nuisances from his wife's range.

It was curious how the relationship, which began with him arranging trysts with Miriam in France or Greece or Honduras (amazing, the number of conferences and seminars they managed to be at, together, in those first years), ended with each one moving independently to foreign capitals and provinces, but never together. Well, perhaps not so curious. Perhaps it was all too predictable. Charlie remembered a movie he had seen in his early years, where an American JP who had married six couples and then, after performing the ceremonies, discovered her licence of authority was post-dated a week or something. The couples she had joined officially were contacted, a year, or several years, later. The comedy was how each relationship had altered. Charlie remembered only one of them: the twosome who buzzed with words, laughter, wit and repartee as they finalised their hasty marriage. When contacted later, they had hardly a word to say to each other.

There had been rough patches but Miriam and Charlie had eventually found a sort of settlement, in the times when they were together and one of them not on some overseas commitment. They played chess (bridge was never mentioned) and concentrated on the moves and the game, but it was companionship, and they were fairly evenly matched. That made a difference.

They had finally come to their balance, an equipoise that gave Miriam all her rights and her freedoms but which did not commit Charlie to a janitor status. In his own world he still had some standing, some credibility, and had begun to adjust to the easier pace, while taking on some contract work. There had been enough of that to reassure him. They had even talked of a joint trip to Spain, which their old friend Bob continually urged on them. 'You both used to be at your best when you were haring around together, like naughty schoolkids,' he kept saying.

So that Miriam's death halfway through her Amnesty International Congress in Thessaloniki sent everything flying. It came out of the blue, and it had such a sudden finality Charlie at first could not believe it. The onrush of decisions, arrangements and activity soon overtook his shock and had him busy as he had not been since his retirement, two years before.

Now there would be no shared experiences, no mockery

of the pictures in hotel rooms, or the inadequate towels, or the supposedly wonderful coffee.

It was twelve months before all the incredible junk and mess had been cleared, allocated, disposed of, or salvaged. The house had been tidied and repainted. It realised a surprising amount at the auction, though Charlie had been unable to force himself to attend. There had been three moves before, three previous auctions, and each one came back to haunt him. The new one was to be distant, impersonal, and Charlie had resigned himself to whatever he could get. The reserve had been minimal, and that only at the agent's insistence. The property leapt past the reserve at the first bid, he was told.

Short term investment of the proceeds was something within Charlie's old line of business. He was left with time on his hands. After settlement, he looked at the remaining furniture and sent off the lot to a secondhand dealer 'in deceased estates'. It was one of those decisions he knew he would regret later – but he also knew he would regret even more having to live with the pieces they had purchased together, or had each brought over from previous lives, previous commitments. No. The lot. Cedar and mahogany had lost their tang, they had a way of reinventing past moments, quite precisely, quite ruthlessly.

The glass fronted double bookcase: Charlie had initially bought that as his first real antique and it was laughable to think what he had paid for it, but even at the time he had rejoiced at the bargain and couldn't have cared less about the little old widow who had put it up for sale because she was being moved to a retirement village. All these years later, her anguished face and her stoop, her stuffy living room and the immense clutter of painted plates, antimacassars, balloon-back chairs and velvet drapes came back, vivid as yesterday. Also the way he beat her down, pointing out the bulk of it, its heavy presence in the room, and the wobbly overmantel, as well as the missing keys that made it useless to lock. 'You'd be lucky to get a hundred pounds in Big White's Furniture,' he had said. It was now worth five thousand.

Ghosts. No, out with them all. Everywhere he looked, even with so much of the household furniture already sent off to children, in line with Miriam's will, and with all those 'might come in handy' bits and pieces (from long pieces of timber to what seemed like every piece of electric gadgetry ever invented) at last bequeathed to the Salvos, in each room of the house Charlie still found himself looking into a mirror, not a tunnel, of remembering. And what made it worse, each memory associated with each stick of furniture or property was as if each moment of the past were still now. Everything lived still in a perpetual present tense. He had not realised that furniture had this power.

The afternoon the carrier came to remove the contents, Charlie at last knew this part of his life was ended. He had arranged one week's accommodation in a rather comfort-able old hotel in the city, it was the one where he had fairly regularly had a Friday afternoon G & T with some of the remaining work associates from the old days.

He had cleared out the furniture, he had sent to the tip a remarkable volume of paperwork, he had even thrown out all those albums of photographs – though at the last moment he had torn out twenty or thirty pages, sufficient to allow himself some moments of sentimental reverie if the mood should overtake him, though he remained suspicious of himself for this indulgence. He had discarded nearly all his old clothing, suits and vests, some shoes not worn for a decade, those ridiculous T-shirts with their witty forgotten images and sad language, and a drawerful of socks, ties and underwear. It was summer, and winter things like woollens and over-coats were useless now. Charlie had thoughts of moving into a warmer part of the country. He already had made enquiries – with stimulating results – about the prices for home units

on the Sunshine Coast of Queensland. His family had holi-
dayed at Caloundra for five or six years in a row when he was
in the first years of adolescence. Strange, how something like
that, after all these years – fifty or so – came back, surfaced,
and filled him with a sort of old anticipation. It was the old
energy and the excitement that, curiously, tingled.

He could remember his father's old car and the crowd
of them, all singing the radio commercials of the day and
urging Dad to overtake, overtake. His father had been dead
forty years.

Perhaps it was the swirl of curious memories that had
been stirred up by the shift and displacement of all the old
furniture. Caloundra. Those had been glorious times, and
the coastline there so impressive, so various: rock cliffs with
pandanus palms scrambling among basalt rocks, the beige
sandy beaches and all that repetitive and hypnotic surf, the
Stillwater of the Passage, where Bribie Island had its northern
tip within swimming distance from the mainland (except
that the rip was always too dangerous, even when they had
been swimming champions). The wildflower plains, always
full of Christmas bells in December when they came up.
The small village itself, solid and squat and settled, with its
permanent residents – fishermen, farmers, retired weather-
beaten teachers and clerks. They had called it a Graveyard
Town, in those days. Well, here was Charlie at last, ready
to be one of the retirees, and it was a strangely consoling
thought. He was coming home.

+++++

Beatrice had been really his brother's friend. She was family,
in the way that so many people in their wide circle were
'family'. Her parents had lived next door until Beatrice was
seven or eight and then had moved to another suburb, but
the parents had remained in touch and Beatrice, once or

twice a year, came over. She was familiar company, taken for granted. So that the year Beatrice came up to Caloundra with them for the summer holiday was just an added one to the number. Her father had just died and it was decided that this was the ideal way 'to take Beatrice out of herself'. They always rented the same large house, Pen Y Sarn, on the headland overlooking the Passage and it had lots of rooms and the big turn-around verandah-sleepout where the boys and their friends could batch down. Beatrice was to share the big inside room with Jane, Charlie's elder sister. Inevitably there were three or four of the three boys' friends included; Charlie's mother wisely recognised that house guests were a great bonus – bickering and sibling rivalry tended to be deflected, chores like washing up and drying could be made group activities, and they could all go off in a gang to the beach or the island or hire a dinghy for the day and go fishing. Even going to the one cinema with its canvas seats was done in a spirit of adventure and complaints were minimal.

The year Beatrice joined them, and a couple of their other friends, Charlie was just fifteen. Jane welcomed another girl in the gang; until that year she had always refused to bring one of her own friends; 'the boys are too rowdy, no thank you, I wouldn't submit Katrina or Ellice to that!' Jane always joined in everything, though, and didn't put on airs. Beatrice, nearly two years younger than Jane, turned out to be as big a tomboy, except when the two of them got together in their room and talked seriously about fashions and film stars and hair styles. By half way through the summer holidays both Jane and Beatrice had wild salty hair and peeled noses.

That was the year Charlie discovered that girls were special.

+++++

The upstairs pub turned out to be not a good idea. Charlie was bored, restless, and the sad impersonal room was worse than the least appetising pensione in Venice or Bologna. Charlie found himself down in the bar more often than he was used to, but even the bartenders were a different shift and of course none of his old mates appeared, except at 5.30 on Friday, as if they, too, had come straight from work.

He drove out past the old house only once. This is nonsense, he thought. Be resolute.

He amassed a number of glossy brochures, not only of units on the Sunshine Coast in Queensland, but at Yamba, and Forster, and Gosford and even Sorrento – though the warmth had, metaphorically, seeped into his bones and windswept southern beaches held no attraction. In his mind's eye his toes were making their old explorations through the warm, gritty sand of Caloundra with its inviting texture like decomposed shellgrit and its clean but auburn colour – not like the white bone nakedness of the Gold Coast but heavier and close under the feet, almost friable.

He and Miriam had gone to the beach at Sorrento only once, decades back. A relentless westerly, stinging water and stinging sand too: they had crouched in borrowed windcheaters and Charlie had peeled orange prawns and put them, one by one, into Miriam's mouth until they finally gave up and retired to the glazed windows of the kiosk where he had bought the prawns. They ended up eating greasy potato chips and slurping bad coffee, comparing disaster beaches in Mexico and on the Aegean coast.

All the home units offered appeared to be made almost entirely of glass and rust-resistant but vulnerable looking metals. Charlie suspected aluminium. Inner walls were almost certainly concrete slabs, papered or painted. Jacuzzi abounded. All promised fabulous views, some of them so close to the water it was as if nobody had bothered about possible beach erosion or cyclones. The pile of discards grew, and the latitude inexorably moved northward.

The Gold Coast did tempt. One eighteenth floor unit overlooking the white extended beach (and all the neighbour high rise units across the road and along the strip) boasted it also had fine views back to the ranges, Springbrook and Binna Burra, and the Macpherson range with Mount Warning. Charlie remembered that time he and Miriam discovered the mountain pool up there, deep in the ferny underbrush and with its huge glossy rocks and precipices. There was a waterfall, cold and almost black behind the white froth of its activity. They had swum, naked, and screamed at the chill of the water, then they had picknicked and sunbaked languidly, deliciously free and private but aware that perhaps less than a kilometre away there was the main road and sweating tourists stuck to their fixed maps. It had only taken a little detour and the attraction of a small dirt road which, in a moment of random daring they had turned into and, voila, their own special rockpool and waterfall. That had been in the ecstasy days of their partnership.

It seemed the obvious thing. Charlie booked a flight up to Coolangatta. He would get a hire car and be practical. After all, he might yet decide, for convenience, on an apartment in South Melbourne.

+++++

Beatrice had been, from the outset, the star. She led the rowdy singing around the kitchen sink during chore-time, she whipped up her own special malted-milk drinks from café-style grooved glasses and with long stemmed spoons to scoop up the ice-cream from the bottom. The glasses and the spoons were her gifts to the family, for having her. The malted milks were her own invention. Charlie still remembered (with a certain astonishment) his particular Beatrice-favourite: coca-cola flavoured milkshake. Would that have been possible? What were the other Beatrice-flavours? Mango milkshake, which had astounded everybody – such a combination had seemed almost bizarre, mangoes were what you slurped out over the back stairs, dribbling their acid sweetness over your wrists. Today, of course, mango flavoured ice cream was everywhere.

Beatrice had also persuaded Jane to help her with her very special Christmas cake, which used unheard-of quantities of nuts and glazed cherries and raisins and almost no actual cake, just enough rich brown paste to bind it all together. It was memorable, an instant hit.

Years later, in Adelaide, Charlie had gone with Miriam into Ditters where they bought small and highly priced replicas of exactly the same Beatrice-cake (as the family traditionally called it). He had asked the woman behind the counter if she knew the origin of the recipe. 'Old Mrs Ditters saw it in an *Australian Woman's Weekly* years ago', she said. 'It was, I believe, an American recipe.'

In his heart, if not in his voiced expressions, it remained still Beatrice-cake.

Miriam had fingered a small piece, but put it aside. Charlie placated her with a box of chocolate coated macadamia nuts.

How many other 'traditions' had their genesis in that first Christmas with Beatrice? Charlie found he could not think of Shelley Beach without her somehow present. Though, on their earlier holidays, they had been exploring for shells on that rocky, pool-miraculous stretch. It was Beatrice, of course, who had found the unbroken Nautilus shell, cast up on the one small turbulence of sand between the rocky cliffs and the jumble of basalt tors, 'ancient volcanic activity,' their father had said.

The Nautilus was much prized, but at the end of the holiday

Beatrice had presented it to Jane. By that stage Charlie felt he had a certain precedence. He had been astonished.

+++++

Coolangatta airport was full of families in Hawaiian colours with brown faces. Even the tribes of children looked bulky, and their inevitable clutter of surfboards, backpacks and gaudy luggage like sausages from a Purple People Eater, left Charlie pushed into a corner, as if there were a corner in the huge hangar of a building. But the Purple People Eater did amuse him, gallumphing out of his memories of those teenage 'novelty songs' they had so loudly yodelled in those holiday years. 'The Naughty Lady of Shady Lane', and 'Ghost Riders in the Sky' had been favourites, but the former only because Beatrice had brought the sheet music with her and sang it with her almost husky voice. 'Ghost Riders' was one the boys liked – but not the Bing Crosby version. Charlie collected his small Qantas Frequent Flyer black travel bag from the carousel and moved out to the Hertz hire car booth, humming quietly to himself.

He had booked no accommodation. That was the new relaxed man. In the years of his constant overseas travel, Charlie always nursed a tight coil of anxiety until he had organised accommodation for at least a week ahead. Miriam was utterly careless, and always seemed to come upon quaint little hotels or pensiones or even serviced rooms and chalets. She passed the details to Charlie but inevitably if he arrived in Vienna or Amsterdam or wherever, some months or years after Miriam had discovered her special hideaway, it would be fully booked, or under renovation, or would turn out to be a fifth floor attic with no heating and a view of lead-roofs or down into some stables or factory. He had begun to suspect that Miriam tended to glamorise her little 'discoveries'.

Though he avoided the glassy international hotel chains, Charlie ended up booking ahead through Qantas, telling himself that the cost was, after all, income tax deductible.

To drive through the highway north, towards Surfers and Southport was to be suddenly swirled in a double series of shocks. One shock was to recognise small locations out of his childhood past – that row of Norfolk Island pines north of Kirra looked exactly the same size as when he had been initiated into the mysteries of alcohol at eighteen, lurching out to vomit under, surely, precisely that same pine across the road from the hotel. The hotel itself was still there, but completely altered. That was the other shock: the streets and layout were remarkably preserved, but the actual buildings: that was another thing! Where he remembered fibro cottages on stilts or brick-veneer bungalows set in big lawns with perhaps a mango or frangipani as the only gardening evidence, now the whole strip was bricked up into apartments with concrete slab patios and rusting iron railings, or the occasional Tuscan villa, all white porticos and tubs of bougainvillea.

The new highway cut through the back of the hill at Currumbin and it was at that moment Charlie knew he could not settle here, on the Gold Coast. It had become overgrown and overbuilt, but it had been always so. Before the building booms of the sixties, seventies, eighties and nineties this whole strip had been largely sand and marram waste, or ti-tree scrub and wilderness. He remembered no Christmas bells in this stretch. Surfers' Paradise itself had an entirely naked foreshore, bitumen and then shops and the Surf Lifesavers' Club. He recalled times when they returned to their cars (in the years when they had graduated to cars) and the seats were so hot they had to throw their damp towels across them before they scrambled in, avoiding the metalwork and commiserating with whoever was driving, as he attempted to handle the steering wheel with whatever was at hand – one of the girl's caps, or a tangled handkerchief or the shammy from the glove box.

Brisbane itself produced an ache to the very heart. Was it just three years ago when he had last been in the city? But that was a passing visit and he had been driven directly from the new airport to St Lucia and the University, so much of it old familiar territory. It was surprising how the city of his mind had been defined by trees, specific trees. If they were still there, then stability of a sort was assured. If some roadway project or building site had demolished some avenue or tree he remembered, then the whole area had been ruined by concrete, high rise, greedy speculation. The flourishing green suburbs around St Lucia restored his belief in mankind, Charlie felt. He remembered a botanist friend, many years ago pointing out that there were now more flowering native trees, like callistemon or buckinghamia or bauhinia, than at any time before white settlement.

Coming from the Gold Coast, the new roads were confusing and Charlie became aware that the city of his boyhood could now only be traversed by referring to maps and directions. He was across and onto the Bruce Highway before he realised it. As he had moved, so glidingly and swift, up the coast highway he had been contemplating an overnight stay in the city. There were a few friends and acquaintances he might look up, surprise them with a phone call and an offer of a meal somewhere. He assumed that even Brisbane possessed a few tolerable eating houses by now. His last memory, of a meal at Lennons, still coated his palate with mayonnaise and quickly unfrozen prawns, overripe beef and greasy baked potatoes.

Miriam had been with him that time, it was one of the few occasions they had intersected – Miriam for a seminar at the Princess Alexandra and him for a week's research in the Oxley Library. They had chosen Lennons because Miriam remembered her first 'grand meal' there with a business

friend of her father when she had ordered Bombe Alaska
to the horror of her parent and the delight of the business acquaintance, who was paying. Lennons, during the
Second World War, had been the headquarters of General
MacArthur and the American military presence. It had been
a cornerstone. The time Charlie and Miriam made their
'sentimental journey', Lennons had been demolished and a
substitute high rise hotel erected over in Queen Street. They
should have been warned. The dining room was a revolving
affair on, presumably, the top floor. You looked out on the
lights of other buildings.

But they had laughed, later, and they reinvented almost
childish delight in the fripperies of their bedroom, turning
on the television and ordering up champagne and a snack of
something unmentionable like tacos and Miriam had stuffed
Charlie's toilet bag with all the shampoo, conditioner, soap
and cottonbuds on hand, while Charlie had placed the shower
cap upon her head and swathed her in the big white towel-
ling robe. While Miriam reclined in sartorial splendour on
the queen-size bed, Charlie had strolled naked to the door
when the waiter appeared with the tacos and champagne and
then elegantly scrawled his signature on the chit. Miriam
described to him in detail, later, exactly the range of expressions on the young man's face.

It was when he found himself crossing the Storey Bridge
that Charlie realised he had lost it. Not worthwhile turning
back into the downtown part of the city now. Funny, it seemed
almost irreligious to refer to the city centre, curved into
the armpit of the Brisbane River in one of its wide loops, as
'downtown'. Such an American term. Brisbane had been the
most Americanised of Australian cities during World War
Two. Charlie still remembered stopping Yank servicemen
for chewing gum. Quite blatantly. And they always obliged.
Most of them were not all that much older than Charlie's
eldest brother, had he thought of it. But they were so imbued

with glamour and spending power that no comparison was ever made. Coffee was introduced with the Yanks. And avocado. And waffles, but who ate waffles now? With Maple Syrup? And jeans. Charlie was the first in his family to come home with a pair of blue jeans, it must have been 1950, 1951. He had worn them up on the holidays at Caloundra that year. And the rayon lairy shirt. He had been the first of the boys to wear rayon, too, and in those technicolour hues: yellow and orange and red. There was a photograph, still, of him standing on the top of a dune over on Dicky Beach near the wreck of the ship that was submerged in sand. Looking so cocky and full of himself, and he had been. Beatrice, he remembered, had taken that snap.

No. The photograph was no more. It was one of the thousands he had consigned to the fire. And what need to keep all that memorabilia? See, he thought to himself, I can draw it up from my own memory, clear as any visible evidence. Clearer, if the truth be known. Photos cannot carry the resonance. At most, they can only hint at it, or falsify as often as not, including details irrelevant to the point, or placing a perspective on things as if even the big moments were only relative. He remembered, still, the painful disappointment when photographs were returned from the chemist, and all the figures were too far away, or too small, or dwarfed by objects not even intended – that other couple on the sand dune, not even noticed at the time. Or that other photograph of Beatrice taken that Christmas, when he had particularly wanted to catch her delight as they all crowded round the picnic hamper Mum had prepared specially the day they hired the boat over to Bribie. She had pickled pork, which was Charlie's favourite, and all sorts of things in aspic – tinned asparagus and beetroot and peas. By the time they settled to the picnic lunch the aspic was dangerously gelid but the pork was a triumph. Beatrice was delighted with the aspics and promised to try the recipe when she got home, it would be just the thing for her unhappy mother on those hot summer days. The photograph had turned out as a muddle of faces, too many of them, and you could not even make out the picnic things. Nor Beatrice's happy laughter, just a sort of smirk under her shady sun hat. It was the sort of photo that should be tossed right away. Charlie had kept it in his album all these years, as if it could be even an aide-mémoire. Well, it was that. But it had long lost any relevance or even intention. The last time he had actually looked at that particular set of holiday snaps was when Julie, his daughter, dragged them out. And that was only to laugh at the grotesque fashions of another era.

Pickled pork. Well, that had really been years back. Hard even to remember what it tasted like. Salty and soft, perhaps? So many things had changed, so many things had improved. Those meals his mother had so strenuously prepared in the family kitchen over the stove – and even over the wood stove in Pen Y Sarn. Nobody would contemplate such slavery today. And certainly not such stodge!

Miriam had shocked him deeply, that time in Lennons, when for breakfast, again delivered to their room, she had wolfed down a large plate of bacon and eggs.

He was driving through northern suburbs of Brisbane now, crossing corners and streets suddenly familiar with an ancient tiredness, or broken and transformed with super-markets and glassy offices or emporia, but he noted the shallow, flat neighbouring streets and on the low stunted ridges the eternal Queensland houses, in timber and faded paint, louvres and creosoted slats imprisoning the under-the-house, and always with straggling fences and wide, dry grass blocks with acalypha, allamanda and scrawny rose bushes, and shrubby, stalky street trees, no higher than the garden gate most times: bauhinia again, bottlebrush or shrivelled mela-leuca. The hot parched summers of his boyhood returned. The humid afternoons waiting for an evening thunderstorm.

The times spent hosing, in the afternoon glare, his mother's hibiscus or the fruit trees, or the vegetable patch behind the kitchen. None of the new monstrosities or the glossy facades of supermarkets or Branch Headquarters could disguise that old familiarity. Why had he even thought of returning to these tired streets with their memories of heat, of boredom, of a perpetual sense of nothingness?

Well, he had left all that behind, and life indeed had been more busy and more memorable even than he would have imagined in his boyish dreams. It had been with its miseries too, but somehow even disasters and mistakes and damn silly decisions proved those old boredoms were simply part of adolescence. Perhaps young men everywhere, no matter how rich the environment around them, are tugged into those afternoons of indirection and self-demoralisation. It is called growing pains. It has to be universal.

Suddenly he was into the real countryside. Once he had crossed the Pine River things became greener, lusher, the trees higher, the hard glittering ridges replaced by water meadows and a vegetation that he recognised as he had recognised those bleached suburbs. But it was a recognition that promised abundance. He recalled those long drives up to Caloundra and the highlights along the way: the first sight of the Glasshouse Mountains rising like solid ikons from the plains and with the long row of timbered mountains beyond. The huge forests of pinus radiata that followed the Bruce Highway – ecologically deplorable, he knew, but massively impressive – as well as the edges of real rainforest, impenetrable still and alluring, a thick melee of leaf shapes and dense shadows fringing the road and stretching back he never knew how far: if they had retained at least a token of these, he would be satisfied. Revived and satisfied.

The new road was smooth, divided lanes and almost before he knew it Charlie was into the area of the Glasshouse Mountains, and paused, and wondered yet again, before he pushed on. Why did they hold him so? They were presences. They were more than that, they were like manifest expressions of all his growing up, of all the growing up of himself and his brothers and sister, of his parents even, and no doubt of generations earlier, much earlier into the Dreamtime of the original tribes in this area. Things to be worshipped, and to remain Other.

Then the stretch, before the Caloundra turn off: that vast wilderness of forest, despite the highway, was there still, and he could not explain even to himself the satisfaction that gave him. Turning the loop and into the flats and hillocks of the Caloundra road, Charlie glanced back. The ranges rose and swelled and were green and fertile around him. Though he had never actually said it, they were among the most beautiful landscapes he had ever seen. And he had seen many. A quiet exhilaration descended upon him and even though it was early evening now and he would make Caloundra before dark, he found himself driving slowly – so slowly other motorists honked and overtook at risky intervals – as if he were reabsorbing some spirit of place that he had once been connected to but which had become lost to him. He had forgotten the Gold Coast utterly. Brisbane was merely an interruption, as perhaps it had always been. Though this area had only been a holiday site, a place of interruption from the worries of real life, yet it had its own powers. The powers of recuperation, as they used to say; but it was more than that.

It was, surely, a country that had entered deeply into his unconscious soul and perhaps it had never left that place. He could not have contemplated return here, certainly not as a permanent measure, at any time in his life before. Charlie recognised that. But now so many things had been discarded, or lost, or removed from him, in this stripping down of expectations and hopes, as well as in this building up of thoughts and alternatives, he had something to come back to, and that was a sort of bonus. He had something to rediscover.

Something to reinvent perhaps, but something where those previous negotiations had made preparations, preparations he himself had never fully realised.

He recalled his retired uncle and aunt, in their little cottage near Bulcock Beach, all those years back. He had never envied them. He had, rather, thought on them with a sort of mordant pity, locked into their minute world of card games in the evening, and endless fishing in the Passage, and an afternoon walk up to the corner store for milk, or sugar or tobacco. What a sad life it had seemed. Now he was not so sure.

Two

Westaway Towers was the first high rise set of apartments in Caloundra. Built in the 1960s, its fifteen floors still stand out although the high ridge beyond the town centre and Bulcock Street is now glistening with glass and sundecks. Westaway Towers looks solid, though, its three-bedroom apartments half shut off from the sun by white barricades and viewing slits. You can look out at the distance in Moreton Bay with its big sand island sometimes visible. This is not forefront property, it sits on the rocky ridge where a seedling Moreton Bay Fig has set roots into the unwilling stone and is now twenty-five-feet high, and is the home of a family of magpies, no doubt cruelly territorial in the nesting season. Charlie found it almost ridiculously easy to purchase one of the flats.

They were old fashioned, which he liked. Solid timber fittings in the kitchen, no veneer or laminex, and the bathroom tiles and accessories must have been modish forty years ago. They still had class. He was able to get vacant possession almost immediately, and at a ridiculously low price. Cash, of course. He had spent a week buzzing round the awful strip towards Maroochydore looking for essential furnishings and the necessary bits and pieces, nothing more than perfunctory. It was as if he could not in any sense replicate the specifics of their old home. He congratulated himself again and again on his decision to clear the lot. No reminders.

A set of plain white crockery from The Reject Shop Warehouse, fitted sheets – essential things like beds, mattresses and a truly dreadful lounge suite came with the deal. Charlie picked and pecked for the minimum gadgets, and a television, and filled in the appropriate forms for phone contact, the power reconnection, all of it without thinking, almost.

It was not until he had been there over a week that the running stopped. He was alone.

In all that long period since Miriam's death, activity had claimed him. Wonderful how whole months can be filled with meetings and appointments, visits to banks and solicitors and insurance offices, antiquarians and secondhand dealers. Then the cleaning and overseeing of the entire house and premises. In all that time it had been a matter of deadlines and the inexorable sense of pressure to have it all properly and cleanly organised. He had done so much himself. It had seemed fitting.

Only the necessarily meticulous sorting out of papers and memorabilia had been truly painful, but he had prepared himself for that and, in the end, even the more personal things were tossed. It was an accelerative process, and once he got under way, there was almost a reckless fury that developed, as if he could not throw everything out quickly enough. He remembered his own father, so many years ago, who in his final years spent hours down in the backyard incinerator, in the years when burning off was still possible. At the time, he had argued with the old man, and even salvaged a driving licence dated 1922. His father had laughed, and had shrugged and let him keep it. It had long since vanished – otherwise, Charlie realised, it would have ended up with all his other junk, headed for the tip or burned in his living room grate.

Aunt Minnie, when she died, left everything in her cottage, from balls of string and unused pieces of soap to carefully ironed Christmas paper and dullish baubles from the tree that Charlie remembered himself helping her to decorate. He must have been nine when she died. His mother had looked over the house, picked at a few Doulton plates and the like, and then called the Salvos to remove the lot. Charlie had even considered that tactic this time, but there was a certain necessity to go through everything, to eliminate things carefully. Eliminate them he did.

He was sitting on the lumpy lounge chair in front of the *7.30 Report*, on his eighth night in the flat and his third week in Caloundra when it happened.

The happenstance and inveterate peripatetic nature of their professional lives had meant that though each of them had been long accustomed to being alone, in transient rooms or in their own house, each of them also knew the other was there. Within email or phone contact usually. A voice and a shared presence, even during the absences.

After the immediate shock of Miriam's death, that absent presence had not really been displaced. Even as Charlie opened her drawers and fingered her underwear and her jewellery or her hoard of office files and her prodigious correspondence folders, it had been like conversing with her, sharing old memories and occasions, joint celebrations or the specific times she had read aloud to him Nanette's ribald letters or those deeply pompous annual epistles from her Uncle Hymie. Tossing all that had been, not an act of sacrilege, but a sort of final salute.

Final.

Now it was done. There was nothing to do any more. All this time had been filled out with things to be ticked off. They had been, tick tick. The strange room and the space around him seemed abnormally empty. He was truly alone.

+++++

Grief overtook him. Sitting before the television with its reports of distant calamities, his own almost impossibly distant bereavement caught up with him. There was nothing in the place to comfort him. The used furniture reeked of other lives and other holidays and alternative relationships, now surely ended as well. When he first moved in he had imagined, almost playfully, the old widow eking out her last decade, housebound, bored with the views, maintaining a hollow ritual of vacuuming, sweeping, polishing and cooking a proper meal, only for herself or the very occasional married son and his family. He had seen her as the relict of a fleshy solicitor in Brisbane, who had connections with the building contractors who had made the initial risky venture, getting in at a special price. The furniture was certainly holiday weekender stuff, though there were a few hints of class: the built-in mirror cabinet for the display porcelain, the hidden stereo set. When they retired permanently here the husband had intended to do a lot of rock fishing, and to join the local bowls club. His stroke had curtailed all that, and left the widow to fill out another decade or more, wiping over the china and preparing those regulation meals, three veg and the proper gravy.

Her stroke.

Miriam had emailed him the night before: 'After I give my paper I will take time off for a more intensive examination of the Philip of Macedon treasures. Did you remember to put the rubbish out Tuesday night? There is a general collection week after next but you could go through the potting shed and the laundry, there must be some things we can abandon, but I should be back the day before so I can give it a proper lookover. Luv, M'.

Every word.

The emails stopped. No phone calls – only the terrible one with the news; a hysterical fellow conferencee who had knocked on Miriam's door in the morning to ask about her own paper. Later, it was established that Miriam had taken a seizure in the shower, the water was still running (by now cold) when Lorna poked her head in, discovering the door unlocked. Hours.

It was not morbidity, it was with a sort of deep tenderness and concern that Charlie now attempted to imagine that last event. It was something he had not been able to bring himself to contemplate before; the news, and the shock, and the sudden surge of arrangements that tumbled upon him made such a thing impossible. Over the phone he had been careful to establish that all of Miriam's things were at hand: her watch, the three bracelets and the amber beads, her leather purse with the credit cards and the smaller one with bank-notes and travellers' cheques, her passport. Her passport; it was one of the very few things he had not abandoned, it had not been cancelled yet – when would some clerk somewhere take note and file a requisition?

With the osteo Miriam had always been careful about the shower. He hoped to God the stroke had been utter and instantaneous. Too much to contemplate Miriam sprawled awkwardly at the base of the tiny shower recess, perhaps with her legs twisted under her, and still breathing, attempting to scrabble for some support or means of reaching her purse and the mobile phone, which she would certainly have taken into the bathroom, her usual precaution. And the water still pelting down on her, like needles by this time. No, no gain in thinking along those lines. Think only the finality of it.

The finality.

Finality for Miriam. For himself the endless series of urgencies and activities to bring everything to a completion. To have the funeral and the ceremonies properly organised. Organisation: that was his thing, Miriam had always agreed. He had not broken down, not once. Miriam's daughters were harrowing enough, even his own daughter, who had always been guarded about Miriam, Clinging to his arm, she had gone to water. Later, she had whispered, 'How will you manage, on your own, Dad?' But then she had added, 'Though you've had lots of practice.'

Practice cannot be compared with the real thing. The real thing comes with a sense of absolute finality. Until this point, Charlie had too much on his hands to have them removed, and the sense of complete vacancy descend. Hands? There were no hands. Feet, body, hair, face. Face: there was no face, no voice, no flash or eyes or that sudden, almost majestic laughter.

Gone. Taken.

At some point he realised the tears were streaming down his bristly face, that he was gagging and retching with grief, whole dollops of it. He staggered from the awkward chair and lurched toward the television, fumbling for the automatic controls which he would never remember to take from the console. The noise faded and the images blurred into nothingness. But his eyes still seemed drowned in their own ocean and he realised that a loud deep wail had risen from his mouth, or from deep in his body somewhere, pushing his thorax to get out. The thought went through his mind that the neighbours must wonder, but even as this intruded on his conscious mind something also reminded him that the organisation of these apartments was so clever and sound-proofed that a whole entrance lobby and the lift and stairwell lay between his flat and the other one on this level. He could make all the noise he wanted.

But it did subside. Even the tears completed their task. Charlie lay in the floral chair, exhausted. He was in a room without character amid the cast-offs of other people's lives, and there was tomorrow and tomorrow and tomorrow, as the Bard said. Even in grief, the cruel mockery of others cuffed him, emphasising his aloneness.

After a while he got up and went to the kitchenette and turned on the electric jug. A shadow of that old widow woman before him in this place mimicked his actions. That he was not the first offered him no comfort, no comfort at all.

Nothing and nobody could replace Miriam and the world of ghosts surrounded him, but they were not necessarily even his own ghosts, nor Miriam's. A sense of strange impersonality did nothing to relieve his grinding ache. If anything, it increased it.

There had not even been a goodbye.

The jug shrieked at him. He turned it off, but did not bother to reach for a mug, or the coffee things, or a herbal tea. It hardly seemed worthwhile.

Too early to go to the bedroom. There was nothing on television. Charlie found himself staring out from the windows, misty with the salt air. Somewhere out in the channel a freighter with dullish lights was moving slowly northward. He stood watching it until it passed out of view, beyond the headland of King's Beach.

There were a few lights below him on the slopes of the hill, but it was not the tourist season and what was most apparent was how many houses, and flats and apartments were darkened. How empty everything was.

+++++

He had a dream. He was on an expedition with someone – 'her' – into the Dead Centre, the heart of Australia, with its red soil and, because it must have been a year of good rainfall, incredibly green growth on the smallish trees and shrubs. The shrubs were flowering: golden. The pair of them were rejoicing in the space and open vastness of the landscape, there was a long purple ridge of mountains in the distance and, closer to hand, a sitting-down place, with a pool and white-trunked shade, a billabong. That was when he noticed the survey pegs. He looked further, with increasing concern. The whole landscape had been divided and turned into small allotments, already signs appeared, with FOR SALE and FIRST OWNER'S BARGAIN and GET IN NOW WHILE PRICES ARE LOW. Everywhere he looked, there were already glittering Toyotas and besuited salesmen with sheaves of papers, maps and plans, and a Home Unit developer selling apartments off the plan. An old Aboriginal man who had been sitting down beside them on the shady sand was grinning and showed them the hundred dollar note he had received, but already the bulldozers were roaring in.

Charlie woke in a sweat, and found himself lying in full sunlight from the window of his new bedroom.

The dream made no sense. Yes it did. It was almost as if Miriam had been with him, but the sense remained that he had made a decision without her; that he had plunged into this new property without proper consideration or time to weigh up the balances. He had been somehow involved in the destruction of the virgin landscape of his dream, something Miriam would never have countenanced.

But it was more than that. Charlie was in the kitchenette, again at the hot water jug, when the connection struck. Last week he had been driving back and forth across that flat stretch north of Caloundra, between the shoreline of sand dunes and along the old wallum heath towards Alexander Headland and the cemented and bitumenised carparks of the ugly builders' paradises – Woolworths, Harvey Norman, the rest. They had been shoved willy-nilly upon what he still remembered as the wildflower plains of his youth. Where there were now oily aisles of glinting cars there had once been Christmas bells; and the other tiny wildflowers had grown there, where it now was simply waste. Hundreds of brick-veneer cottages squatted over what once had been a natural garden of native shrubs and grasses, and none of them had retained the old plants. Instead there were hibiscus from Hawaii, pink and red frangipani from other Pacific Islands, jacaranda trees from Mexico, you name it. The Green Finger Nurseries were crammed with exotics, instant lawn and manicured pot-plants. And Charlie had himself parked in those very lots for his grotty little purchases. Miriam would have had a seizure.

He stopped himself at that.

What he had not yet faced, in his fading recollection of that dream, was that it was not Miriam there, it was Beatrice. The Beatrice who had that time called out to stop the car which Charlie's Dad was driving. Right there on the new bitumen road up to Alexander Headland. Beatrice had clambered over the rough embankment and onto the heathland. 'Look!' she had called, and pointed to the flowering abundance. Charlie instantly clambered out after her, and began tugging at the Christmas bells. But she had stopped him. 'No, Charlie. Leave them be. Just look at them, and let others look. If we take them all, there will be nothing left. Perhaps next year they will already have gone.' Charlie had retained the flowers he had picked, though, and they took them home and put them in a glass milk bottle on the window above the sink, where they lived for only a few days.

Neither of them had fully realised just what a devastation lay in store on that seemingly endless heathland plain.

As he sipped the bitter coffee, standing up to look out the windows (when you sat you could not see above the high ledge; one of the drawbacks of the older style units), he almost marvelled at the vividness of that recall, and realised that this area hoarded, still, those memories that had long been submerged in the wider, wilder worlds of his later life, of their later life, Miriam and himself.

Try as he would, he could not install Miriam into this place. Well, wasn't that the intention? New start? New surroundings.

The grief returned, but not so vocal. There were no hopeless tears. Only the hollowness and the complete purposelessness of things. He found he had been staring out at the same view, from the same angle, for ages now.

Beatrice must be an old woman. Impossible to imagine what would have happened to her, how she would have turned out. He did not even know if she were alive or dead. Down below the built-up artifice of the Westaway Towers' gardens, with their Japanese design – square grassy patches, the reed and lily pond, the ordered stepping stones – an older Caloundra still sprawled, down to the rutted and potholed plaza in front of the old hotel. It was all being bulldozed and reorganised now, but wasn't that where they all went on New Year's Eve that time, for the fireworks and the loud amplified band from Brisbane and the sweaty night air and the post-midnight surf, all of them reckless with the New Year and the future? For most of them the future was another year at school, or forty-nine weeks in the office or the shop (was it still two weeks or three they were allowed off?) and perhaps the big night at the Cloudland Ballroom sometime in July or August. Yes, they were all innocent. The boys with their warm beer bottles in the car boot, the girls egging them on, puffing at Ardath cigarettes and letting their shoulder-straps dangle.

That first sight of Beatrice when she bent over to adjust her sandals and her soft breasts curved outward from the delicate secrecy of her armpit, cupped in by the slipping rim of her bathers.

For the first time in ages Charlie found himself smiling.

+++++

Already certain patterns were being formulated, almost without his conscious control or direction. He found himself walking the half kilometre along the ridge to the little news-agency at the top of Bulcock Street for the the *Australian*. He had not descended to the *Courier Mail* yet, but that would come.

Then, after a few more weeks, he discovered a small café

where he could skim through the paper and have a coffee – long black, not cappuccino. That had been Miriam's morning drink She could spend all morning in a café in Brunswick Street or Lygon, over endless coffees and just the first three or four pages of the *Age*. Charlie had imagined her in Paris or Venice similarly occupied, and Miriam would have known how to soak up the ambience as well as the necessary caffeine. Charlie had always been impatient, a list in his pocket and things that had to be done.

All the things that didn't have to be done.

After his coffee and sometimes even a clunky Florentine, he would stroll down to the front, the Stillwater of the Passage. The line of Norfolk Island pines was still there, out of his childhood, but now streetscaped with a concrete and porphyry walkway right along the front where the channel cut close into the banks (his uncle had once shown him a groper's hole along there) and up behind the little changing room and lifesavers' hut (almost unchanged) to lead higher along to the point, which had now been turned into picnic areas, parking places with little loops of grass around each tree and brick toilets and another changing shed with an outside shower. Beyond that he remembered the sand-duney hillocks with their thin casuarina groves and banksia scrub. From Pen Y Sarn they had trekked through that wasteland to reach the foreshore and the turn that led to the surfing beach. It was now all graded and turned into family playgrounds with shade trees predominating above wooden benches and tables. Attractive in its way. Civilised.

Charlie sometimes would take another rest on one of the benches, leaving the paper on the table and perhaps wandering over to the fence that protected the open beach from small children.

It was a bit of a hike uphill from that point, so Charlie more often walked out onto the sand and stood mesmerised by the endlessly recurring surf. And each time, he thought:

perhaps I should have bought somewhere where the surf itself would be close enough to look at from the balcony. But then he thought: storms, erosion, salt spray and that sticky moistness. And he knew that the slow momentum of the incoming waves would be capable of holding him in a thoughtless drugged stupor, perhaps for hours. Surf was like that.

The surf he remembered from the old holiday years had been something to challenge and stimulate, something you plunged into and caught in an exciting roller. Charlie had been a relentless body surfer.

There were other patterns that began to help fill his day. He had never been a man for breakfast, but now he purchased packets of cereal and mixed them with yoghurt and cut up fresh soft fruit from the greengrocer down past the newsagent.

He began to take a kip after lunch. Memories of those after-lunch rests at Pen Y Sarn were replaced by a simple need, an early exhaustion. Sometimes he lay on his back for almost two hours.

Back then, when their parents closed the door of the main bedroom, the young people would play euchre or dominoes. Charlie had learned his first chess moves. Hot sweltering afternoons before the sea breeze came up with its always welcome agitation and relief. There were occasions he had lain on the side sleepout upon the small chaise-longue that seemed like a reminder of Victorian times.

There was the time Beatrice had snuggled in beside him on that narrow horsehair shelf; they had read Boofhead comics and giggled together, imagining an American world of College Students and baseball and gossipy afternoons over milkshakes. Beatrice fitted under one arm, into his shoulder and he had felt her warm body, enticingly soft against his damp shirt. She had wiggled in her bottom to secure a more stable position. He had crossed his legs to make more space, and to hide his excitement.

The high bedroom in his Westaway flat occupied a north-westerly position but any passing breeze seemed to circulate the air and Charlie, so far, had not considered air conditioning. The subtropical warmth was too full of old associations and it seemed to lave him gently. He remembered days of uncomfortable heat and oppression, when they would get in their togs and bring out the hose in the backyard near the outside dunny, just to cool off. After lunch was not a good time for the surf, and his mother always warned them not to swim after a meal. Was that instruction really valid? He had never thought to question it.

But as he shambled out of the back bedroom he found himself doing the same thing, making coffee – it was something which had become a pattern of his marriage and all the times he and Miriam had been together – and in retrospect, that seemed endless and endlessly linked up together. Three weeks, four weeks, sometimes a month: their separations defined them, but their linkings were less spectacular yet more genuinely constant. They simply slipped into old patterns. Like this business of making yet another coffee, and such a pedestrian coffee, Bushells Espresso, straight out of the jar. When he had been to the small supermarket last week Charlie had quite instinctively picked up the 250 gram jar, though the taste of the thing had never delighted him. It was a taste like old cinders, he had once said. But Miriam had brought over to him the new, unopened bottle, and had shoved it right under his nose, after she ripped off the foil. 'Smell this. Aaah!' she had said, and the promise did seem, for a moment, about to be fulfilled. Smell is always more pertinent than flavour, he had said then, and she had laughed, 'Not more pertinent, more perfidious. Fortunately!'

The coffee tasted bitter, but he did not add sugar, though there had been a time in his life when three spoonfuls had been adequate.

But the long hours until dinner had to be filled. He

decided to take the car out in the afternoons, and make a series of sorties, not too far, but to reacquaint himself with his neighbourhood. Mornings were fine for his walk. He could afford to be a little self indulgent later in the day. He would plan out a series of excursions: Montville, Buderim, Noosa if he felt inclined.

Sitting with maps and a Gregory's, Charlie felt a return of that sense of purpose, and he carefully worked out kilometres, times and potential traffic flows. At this stage he had nothing like a picnic set (there had been three wicker baskets, and an Esky, gone, gone). For his first expedition (not tomorrow, the next day) he would buy something on the spot. Already he was thinking Buderim; the ginger factory there would have some sort of café and no doubt any number of ginger confections. Would he indulge himself in a bottle of ginger in some sort of syrup? Miriam had preferred candied ginger, but he recalled the time when they drove from Caloundra up to Buderim on the back of his cousin's old Willies Knight utility, that had boiled on the way – the radiator and the occupants. But the new ginger factory then was a discovery for them and they returned with three bottles, heavy with syrup. He had broken into the first one on the way back, and Jane complained that her hands were dirty with grease from the back of the ute so Charlie had fed the pieces into her mouth. Beatrice was next.

Yes, Buderim.

The car had not been serviced since whenever. Charlie that afternoon looked into the Yellow Pages and selected a garage at random. In the old days at Caloundra every service station was also a garage. No self-serve then.

The next week, the next two weeks or more had been planned out.

+++++

The following morning Charlie was up early, as if there were an important business appointment lined up. Huh! He laughed at that, as if Miriam in another room would call out, 'And what is it this time?'

But now he was up there was nothing for it. He showered, shaved and completed his toiletries. The bathroom still had that look of foreignness about it. This was the one room where the old widow still kept a ghost hovering. At first it had been almost amusing, when Charlie stripped and he danced and flaunted himself for the benefit of the ghost, or of the old lady. He imagined her still with a sparkle, why not? All the recent Guides praised octogenarian sex, didn't they?

He decided not to make his own breakfast, but to walk down to the village and see what was available. A beachside resort had to have something one off, and he had no intention of walking all the way down to McDonalds.

In twenty minutes he was sitting outside that modern little café on the ground floor of one of the recent high-rise apartments just up from Bulcock Beach, the Stillwater. It was an amiable view in the freshness of early morning. He was suddenly reminded of those very early mornings when some of them would come down here, though there was only a little milkbar and grocery in those days. It was the fresh ripple under his shirt that reminded him. It tightened his nipples, even now.

But whether he wished it or not, the other memories did come nudging in. It was on a morning just like that Charlie had first realised how Beatrice and Alan had become flirtatious. 'Flirtatious' was the term he had used, in his mind back then. Alan was just through his first year uni and had always been, in his younger brother's mind, bossy, even surly. Alan had built his own laboratory under the house and Charlie had been banned from it, right from the outset. Alan allowed only one or two of his schoolfriends entry and though Charlie had (of course) invaded it secretly, it was just chemistry things and dry-as-dust smells. His older brother had become a little more tolerant of him once Alan started at St Lucia, though the tram and bus meant he seemed hardly ever home. Alan was saving up buy his own car.

The only activity the brothers shared, really, was tennis. Alan played for keeps. His stinging serve was formidable but thanks to the Saturday contests Charlie's own game had improved out of hand and he had been awarded a half-pocket at school. Alan's other redeeming feature was his loud laugh. It was infectious, and Alan did have a mad sense of humour. He seemed to be able to memorise limericks endlessly, clean and dirty ones depending on the company. It was, he confided to Charlie in a moment of weakness between matches when they all relaxed in the shade of the hire courts they had booked for every Saturday, a way to make conversation with the girls and to break the ice at parties. Alan had started regularly going to parties, in various suburbs.

Alan had suggested the hire court for tennis during that vacation. Great idea. Beatrice paired him in the first mixed doubles. Her game was terrific. It was clear that Alan was impressed: you could tell that by the way he began his string of limericks, which had them in stitches even though Charlie and Jane had heard them all before. Well, most of them.

And then, for Christmas, Beatrice had presented Alan with a book of comic poems, *The Golden Trashery of Ogden Nashery*. Alan was over the roof. 'Ogden Nash is THE comic genius!' he had exclaimed. And all my pals at uni drool over him.' Alan even recited an Ogden Nash poem he had already memorised from one of those uni parties. Before the week was out he had them all by heart also. Beatrice had been transformed from being one of the friends of his kid brother into a smart, sporting type, who was, incidentally, very pretty. Jane had pointed out to the rather dejected Charlie that girls that age – fifteen and sixteen – always had their eye out for older boys, and never, but never, those their own age.

Beatrice still joined Charlie in all his walks and activities, but he did notice how she kept up with Alan now, and was not even quite so close to Jane – who was quite happy to return to her own reading and her habit of designing imaginary garments for some future grand occasion.

No, he had not been jealous of his brother. He knew that Alan would be back with his university friends in a few weeks and this little summer diversion would be forgotten. He, himself, had been awakened sufficiently by Beatrice, who cuddled him all the way back in the car to Brisbane and gave him a very affectionate goodbye kiss at the end, whereas by this stage she gave Jane a peck and Alan a VERY long smile but only a sort of sisterly kiss, like Jane.

Charlie had not understood the nature of all that, and he had not really encountered Beatrice again, except in the distance when he partnered someone (who?) in the Debutante Ball two years later. By this time Beatrice was a truly radiant beauty and was surrounded by admirers. Charlie had waved, and for an instant her smile back had spurred him, but the men around her were so much older and he remembered Jane's warning. She had passed out of his life.

Now, sitting over his second cup of coffee and the brick-like raisin toast that he had allowed to spoil, he found himself stirring more sugar, and he gave a harrumph and pulled himself out of the slouching position. The young Italian hovered while he paid the bill. He took a brisk walk along the esplanade, already familiar in its new way and with almost no shadow of the old shape it had those years back.

Beatrice, and the memories of Beatrice, had served some sort of purpose, he recognised. They were happy memories. Yes, they had given him back some sort of joviality of spirit, as it were. Some lightness out of the past; even, if he were honest, some sense of his early erotic sensibility, when everything was expectation, anticipation.

Before everything happened.

No, he would not brood. Alan: now how much of all that would Alan possibly remember? Alan had been living in London for thirty years now and his children were prune-voiced little snobs. When Charlie was in London he sometimes – not always – gave Alan a tinkle but it was tacitly agreed he would not go up to Hampstead. Cynthia and Charlie had fallen out rather badly once, when Miriam was 'a new number' as Alan so patronisingly put it in those worst big-brother tones. Cynthia referred to Miriam as 'another Jewish Princess'. Charlie had never forgiven her, and in fact it had been two years before he even made contact with Alan again, though Alan was not the one who had made slurs.

Oh, water under the bridge.

Though he did attempt to reinvoke memories of Beatrice again, as he walked slowly back to his flat, it was suddenly difficult. Alan, as ever, seemed to spoil things, simply by being there.

The sun was getting hotter, very hot in fact. Why had he not thought to bring a shade hat? Trudging along the high crest of the road at last, and looking down at the always soothing expanse of water, sand and the long sweep of the island, Charlie found himself repeating one of the Ogden Nash 'trasheries':

> I give you now Professor Twist,
> A conscientious scientist.
> Trustees said 'He never bungles'
> And sent him off to distant jungles.
> There, by the tropic riverside
> One day he missed his charming bride.
> She was, a native told him later,
> Eaten by an alligator.
> Professor Twist could not but smile;
> 'You mean', he said, 'a crocodile'.

No no. Had he got it all right? But Charlie grinned to himself and recalled the very laughter both Beatrice and Alan bestowed upon him, back then, when he had picked up the new book and read out the first thing that came to hand.

+++++

Three p.m. he judged a good time to make his first small tourist excursion into the hinterland. Buderim was a tiny settlement on one of the volcanic hills that bumped into the ocean just beyond Maroochydore. It had once been a place of small steep banana plantations and small market gardeners, and a few retirees who enjoyed its remnants of rainforest jungle and the amazingly fertile deep red soil, which had proved excellent for hibiscus and dahlias, fruit trees and custard apples. Those little wooden cottages (one or two still with sweltering attics) were worth gold now. When the family first went up there in 1950, 1951, they could not give them away. The ginger had been started as a makeshift alternative to the bananas, when market gluts threatened to kill the market. The farmers had tried coffee between the rows of bananas, with some success, but the ginger turned out to be the winner. It was the only ginger factory outside China, someone had told them. Back then, a few neighbour-hood homes, with their big sprawling blocks, had thickets of ginger and these were sometimes dug up and the roots placed on airing trays (usually corrugated iron sheets) to dry and be used, later, in cooking experiments, though Charlie had never actually witnessed their consumption. Ginger was one of the few exotics you might see in a Queensland kitchen, but generally as a Christmas gift, crystallised and in Oriental bowls, syrupy in bottles.

The ginger factory was a makeshift thing in those days. It was now, Charlie discovered, the full production number. Marketing and merchandising had moved in and everything from drinks to dried was available. Busloads of tourists were thronging through. Postcards and photographers were lined up to tackle the visitor.

Nearby a plant nursery displayed hibiscus in pastel shades, large as dinner plates, in token of the area's fecundity. BMWs and Mercedes crowded the lanes and were already dusted with the red imprint of the area.

Driving past the little primary school with its Arbour Day plantation of hoop pines, Charlie caught a reminder of times past, but sumptuous villas preened above the still breath-taking views, either southward to the long line of beaches, or north overlooking the steep hillside down to the Maroochy River right below and the developing or developed real estate beyond. It was all real estate now.

As Charlie moved back towards his own car, parked rather further away than he had expected, he paused as he was about to cross the road to allow an open topped sports car to glide past. It was filled with several young people, animated and all singing together. The sight of that made him grin, it was so, almost, old-fashioned in its sense of innocence and delight. Did young people engage in community singing any more? Was it perhaps a small church group, and they might be singing New Age religious songs? No, they were in bright colours with lots of brown or tawny flesh, they looked too healthy for that.

As the white car drew past him Charlie took a close look. They were moving slowly, obviously seeking a place to park. He realised that if they wanted, they could take his spot, so he called out and indicated with his outstretched key ring. The car paused, right in the middle of the road. Nobody took much notice, the traffic was so packed any manoeuvring was both inevitable and laborious. Charlie hastened towards his own vehicle.

But as he brought himself awkwardly into the driver's seat (these modern cars! No design sense at all! Not practicable for older people!) and turned on the ignition, some shadow of recognition suddenly struck him.

He wound down the window and tried to twist backwards to look more closely at the occupants of the other car. Its driver gave him a wide wave, then signalled for him to move out and off.

Before he could really gather his thoughts Charlie had done just that. The white sportscar made a neat and very tight jiggle into his old place. Charlie was honked at by another six or seven vehicles piled up behind. He was out and onto the homeward downhill road before he could really consider any alternative.

But the girl in the white car, sitting beside the driver. She had that same black hair, that glowing round face and – this was it, this was the give away – she had Beatrice's wide smile, the teeth and the naturally red lips that seemed almost to push out with her expressive enjoyment.

+++++

When he reached the Westaway Towers Charlie had slowed down, but instead of turning his car into the driveway he paused, reversed, and slowly took the vehicle southwards towards the village. He drove down onto the esplanade of Bulcock Beach, but then he took a further turn and he was back on the road which would lead him to Buderim again. He could not explain. He realised, with perfect clarity, that this was unreasonable. There was not the slightest possibility that the white tourer with its young occupants might still be up there. It must be a good half hour since he left and they would most probably only have stopped for ten minutes, time to poke around, buy a souvenir bottle of something, and whiz on. They were in beach attire and the latter afternoon, after a hot day like this, would have made a plunge in the surf almost obligatory.

By the time he reached the parking position and the area neighbour to the ginger sales centre, much of the heavy traffic had departed. A young woman was wiping down one of the outdoor tables, and there were sparrows impudently pecking at crumbs under her feet.

She looked up and gave him a wave. 'Did you leave something behind?' she said, and he realised he had been noticed. Miriam had sometimes called him Peter Ustinov, something he found not at all amusing.

'Ah … I thought of someone else I needed to buy something for.' There was, of course, not a single soul he could think of to give a jar of ginger to; indeed, he had a deep suspicion that the jar he had already acquired would languish on some back shelf.

'Well, you're just in time. Did you know what you were looking for?'

The question hovered in the air, and Charlie paused an instant, before moving towards the glass display case.

He found himself with another jar, and no momentum. How stupid can you get?

That girl in the car just possibly may have been Beatrice's daughter. Her granddaughter.

They say the likeness is most often something that appears after a missed generation. It would be an interesting speculation.

It was something other than speculation; it was a sort of seismic disturbance, quite unconnected to logic or explanations or generational genetics.

It was as if he had caught sight of Beatrice herself, back then.

The disturbance of the idea settled in with him in the car as he drove slowly back to Caloundra. It was a concept he might almost play with, enjoy for its delicate fantasy and its nostalgia.

Nostalgia was a deplorable indulgence. He had managed very effectively not to fall into the pit of self-reflection and self-pity. Nostalgia was simply not to be allowed in his vocabulary. Keep busy, move forward, do not settle into sentimental platitudes. Nothing can restore the past. 'And just as well.' If he had somehow conjured up Miriam at various moments, that was the natural process of association and reflection. You do not banish these things. But you do not soak in them, you do not sink into the fantasyland of might-have-been. But Beatrice?

This time he brought the car purposefully to the under-cover parking area, he locked the doors and moved to the lobby and the lift well, carrying the two packets and his Gregory's road map and a couple of brochures that he had collected or that had somehow attached themselves to his hands.

That laughing face superimposed itself upon the news-reader on television. He turned the instrument off. He was left with his own thoughts.

+++++

The next morning he had decided to continue his routine, establish it, as it were, as a system, so he walked along and down to the village, purchased the *Australian* and then went further until he came to the little café under the high-rise tower. The waiter recognised him and had his coffee by his elbow almost before Charlie had sat down and organised the disposal of his paraphernalia.

After finishing his bacon and eggs he skimmed through the pages, hovering on the finance section, and then, because there was nothing to do, he folded it over upon the crossword puzzles and drew out his ballpoint. The Quick was so simple he felt ashamed of himself for even bothering, but the Times Crossword was altogether too devious and he resented the time it would take to worry out the patronising clues and their altogether too prissy hints and winks.

He folded the paper again and replaced his biro. Feeling slightly exasperated, he looked around at the other tables, perhaps to see if anyone else had succumbed to the crossword virus, as Miriam had called it. Two slightly overdressed women were leaning towards each other and chatting. A man-and-wife sprawled away from their breakfast things and seemed to be dozing, their faces up to the sun. Charlie instantly thought 'Southerners' with a long-forgotten Queensland proprietorship. It made him smile to himself, but it also made him feel self-conscious and uncomfortable. He picked up his things and made again for the pathway under the old Norfolk Island pines.

As yesterday, he walked all the way down to the end and back again. Once there had been sheds and fishermen's storage spaces, now it was another high rise and restaurant. The smell of long dead fish seemed to hang about that area but Charlie knew he was imagining things.

He strolled along to the little knobby headland and took another seat on a bench, placing his paper and things on the picnic table the bench supported. There was another elderly gent sitting on the other side of the table, fiddling with his pipe and muttering to himself. Charlie looked him over before speculatively casting his eyes to the rip in the channel and the sandy reaches of Bribie. A hang glider was floating over the passage and he followed its movement as if this was the entire reason for his being there.

'Bloody reffo bastards,' the other man suddenly exclaimed. Charlie had not heard the word 'reffo' for, was it, forty years. 'Queue jumpers. Afghan terrorists. Send the lot of them back!' he continued.

Charlie ignored him. The man had swivelled around to face Charlie by this time. He had discovered an ear.

'I tell you, mate, them bastards undercut me, went behind me back and snatched the whole block, cash in full, no worries, paid the lot out and I had already signed the contract.

Signed the contract, mind you, and was heading for the bank to line up the finance. Think that mattered a damn? Not on your life! Not on your life, mate, they was in and cash on the dot. By the time I got back the deal was done. The bloody salesman was grinning he was so jack cocky with himself. Bloody Afghanis or Asians or whatever, they skinned me hollow, and they knew it.'

Charlie did not meet his eye. That made no difference.

'You! What do you think of the refugee business? Do you stand up to them? Do you let them come sneaking in and then taking over? How do you think I feel, having 'em come sneaking in and under my nose? – Under my very nose mind you – under my nose outbidding me with cash on the dot, cash on the dot. I would've started up a nice little fish-and-chips on that rundown site, needed a lot but the position, mate, the position. And what do you think they've done to the place? Go on, what do you suppose they've made of it? A kebab house. A bloody kebab house and you can bet your days it will be stinking and unhygienic. I wouldn't bet on it passing any inspection but you know they bribe the health officers, they've got the departments in the palm of their hands, they come in here saying they've got nothing but I tell you, before you can say Jack Robinson, there they are outbidding you and marching in bold as brass. Bold as brass!' He spat, vehemently.

'Where did you say this place is?' Charlie asked, and he knew instantly that he had made a terrible mistake. There would be no stopping, now.

The man thumped the table and stared Charlie in the face. 'Bloody Alexander Headland, you'd have to be mad to start up a bloody kebab place there, they'll be lucky to last a month. Kebabs! Only a fish-and-chips'd have a ghost of a chance and then only if we got some decent weekends after the holiday season. But I had a plan to develop the site, I'm no chicken behind the ears, I'm not wet there. Six blocks I woulda squeezed onto that site before the regulations made it uneconomical, the fish-and-chips was only a front you know what I mean. But the site is worth it. Was worth it.

'And these people who bought it ...?'

'Who stole it, that's what it was, mate; theft. Bloody fuckin' Afghani illegals, terrorists ...'

'Hold on a bit. What makes you think they might be terrorists, Afghan or whatever?'

'Don't ya read the papers?' He thrust out a hand and rumpled the *Australian* on the wooden bench. 'Don'tcha watch TV? Didn'tcha listen to the talkback radio before the last election? Or are you one of their supporters? Sympathisers? Are you one of the bloody wimps that is calling for more immigration, more migrants, more Afghan terrorists to come and take over the country? You know that they are planning to build mosques right here, in Caloundra? You know that? You heard what they're planning to do with Christians? That's right. It's in their book, they promise to destroy the infidel – that's us, matey – and they have a Holy Jihad against America and if you haven't heard it yet, matey, as far as they're concerned America and Australia might as well be identical. Bloody oath!'

Charlie had picked up his papers and the sun hat. He began moving off, but the older man came round and put a hand on his shoulder.

'I tell you this, mate. It's people like you who'll let them all walk over us, who'll let anyone get in and do what they like. God it makes me blood boil. No guts, no backbone, I know your sort. You know what I call your sort: bloody Chinese Takeaways. That's what you lot are. I can see it in your face, mate, don't try to fool me, bloody teachers and intellectuals, fuckin' left-wing bastards, commo sympathisers. Off ya go, crawl off, I've got your measure. Ya live in one of them tower things, I know it, up from Melbourne is it? Come to lord it over us locals? Well, you can go right home to where you come from. We don't need you here.'

He called out to Charlie's retreating figure, 'Bloody felafel eaters, fuckin' kebab cunts!'

Why hadn't Charlie stood up to him? Why not give him back a bit of his own medicine? The thought was only momentarily appealing. He knew perfectly well there was no point in taking up the cudgels with every passing redneck in Queensland.

Redneck.

The word was out and another realisation had seeped into his consciousness. Had he really forgotten why he had left this state, all those many years before?

It was like stepping back through a mirror. Even the sort of clothing that old idiot had been wearing, it could have come from Henzells Store on Bulcock Street in 1951: flannelette check shirt, the rayon-blend short trousers almost to the knee, the thick, safe belt. Even the hat, no modish Akubra but a sweat-stained brown Trilby, with its indented crown. Pathetic really.

The sting, though, caught in his craw. The old anger.

And to walk away from it. God! That old bigot must be crowing to himself, he must be energised for the whole day with his sense of triumph and self-conviction. Charlie might at least have thrown in a spanner or two to unbalance the old idiot's blind arrogance and spitefulness.

He knew there was nothing he could have said. Not to that one. To anyone? Was this just Queensland? What had he come back to?

+++++

Righteous indignation is all very well but it is a solo thing. Me against you. Us against them. Miriam would have shared every nuance of Charlie's fury, but she no doubt would have come out with some quick repartee. She would have stared the old codger down and laughed loudly at him as he shambled off, tail between his legs, to complain of women and foreigners. Though sometimes Miriam walked away from a confrontation – there was that time with a policeman when she seemed positively abject, Charlie would have bristled! – but, as she later explained, there is no point in wasting your energy when the other party is set in concrete. Still, it rankled. It was the old 'anything for a quiet life' routine.

It was the fly in the balm of his new-found paradise.

And it was true: despite all the little niggles and complaints, he had begun to feel this move, so impulsive, had begun to reveal its own logic. He had been prepared to think of this as being as close to paradise as was gettable. Despite the heat and the insects. Though he remembered real plagues of insects back in the early visits. Sandflies over on Bribie Island, mozzies – the black saltwater mozzies – at dusk, and blowflies in the kitchen. Those big stinging flies out on the sand beaches. Apart from a few mozzies, they had all more or less disappeared. He would not think about how this was achieved, though aerial spraying had begun over the mangrove swamps forty years back.

Let the old codger go, he probably would not run into him again. Or, if he did, he would know to avoid him.

But the idea of crossing the road, in this small village where within weeks he would recognise the regulars, was unpalatable. Perhaps the old man was simply a weekend visitor.

Not likely.

Those young people were where the future lay. It was something of a relief to cast his mind back to the sporty white car and the happy group inside it. They must be looking forward with energy and ebullience, they were the new breath of fresh air in this state. The sour old codger would find his mouth stuffed with cotton wool in their presence, he would slink off and vent his spleen amongst others of his ilk in some tiled public bar or geriatric bowling club.

Charlie had not aged like that. Indeed, if that was old age, he had never succumbed to such defensive plaints and prejudices.

Beatrice looked more than fifteen. Eighteen at the least. Though he remembered how she seemed to grow up suddenly as soon as she and Alan latched on together, at the end of those holidays. She had certainly been, like Charlie, one of the gang, one of the holiday kids at the beginning. That long drive home: Beatrice had sat in the back seat with Alan and there had been that element of maturity about her. They had talked quietly about cinema and compared performances, whereas driving up she had been like the others and only called for the hit songs of the latest movies. The Howard Keel and Cathryn Grayson numbers had been tortured to death. Going home, it had been deep talk about James Mason and Laurence Olivier, Bette Davis and Vivien Leigh. Why was it that false memories of Beatrice snuggling up with him in the back seat of his father's car on that return to Brisbane had initially superimposed themselves on his memory?

But the thought of Beatrice now as an eighteen year old had a warm, fuzzy feel about it, as he would have said with a smirk to Miriam.

Miriam had never even heard of Beatrice.

+++++

It was a week and a half later that he saw her again.

He was just clambering into his car at the back of the little laneway behind the old picture theatre. There was an arcade of shops, hoping for the rush of custom that would be building up in the forthcoming holiday season. He had driven the car down this far in order to carry the groceries and fruit he had decided to stock up on. He was about to put the key into the ignition when he looked up and there, right before his very eyes, she was striding, hand in hand with the sporty young man. They were laughing together and she tossed her black hair. It was exactly the same mannerism Beatrice had developed once she had her hair cut shorter in those weeks of holidays, back in 1951.

Charlie gave a start, took off his glasses and rubbed them, and then quickly got out of the car, forgetting to lock it with its conspicuous brown bundles of groceries.

By the time he had followed them round the corner they were nowhere in sight. He imagined they might have gone into the picture theatre, but he abandoned the idea of following them in. It was a coincidence. He was not tracking her.

But he did look into the real estate agency and the fruit store and a couple of other places, just in case.

He was perhaps a quarter of an hour at most. When he returned to the car his goods were safe, though he suddenly worried about the tub of ice-cream, a rather idiotic choice but it was mango flavour and ancient spices tingled his memory, so he gave in. Likely as not it was half melted. Well, he could throw it out.

She was very much the height he remembered her, and that toss of the head, amazing how suddenly it all returned! That laughing smile, of course, nobody else could have the same expression: the mouth is one of the most idiosyncratic parts of the body.

It would be fascinating to discover her name. There must be some sort of consanguinity, though direct ancestry had to be a real possibility. The real Beatrice, the one he knew, was almost certainly still alive. She may even be living in some sort of proximity? Perhaps this girl was staying with her, in her retirement cottage, in her home unit?

There is no harm in asking a simple question.

He unpacked his goodies and laboriously trudged with

them – all in one go, why bother making two journeys of it, that little set of stairs with their iron rail leading up to the foyer level had already announced themselves as a bit of a hurdle. Then with one desperate finger he managed to press the up button on the lift without losing anything. Getting off at his floor, he had to place them all down before searching for the right key. He would make two journeys this time, in bringing them all in to the kitchen.

The phone was ringing.

By the time he got inside, unloaded the first batch, and reached for the instrument it ceased. Why had he not arranged an answerphone? Now he would spend the afternoon wondering who on earth could be ringing him here? He had not yet got round to preparing a change-of-address circular.

She had been wearing shorts – a sort of pale lemon – and a white top. Her body had grown that little more filled out, almost voluptuous. And she carried herself with that same straight spine and upright bearing – his mother had always been so approving of Beatrice's 'carriage' as she called it. Alan had been a constant stooper in his early years of adolescence, Mum had always been reprimanding him. As he got older of course he reached his full height, which was nearly a foot greater than Charlie (and was one of his sources of envy!). By that stage Alan was getting proud of his height and flaunted it.

With that upright bearing, she had been fluid, not stiff or stilted. Like Alan, in fact, this girl was clearly assured in her bearing. Was she aware that also uplifted the thrust of her breasts? She was a girl maturing quickly into womanhood, and quite at home in her comeliness. Lucky boy, whoever he was!

Well, it hadn't been imagination. That first glimpse, and it had been no more than that, had been entirely accurate. This time he had something like a full minute to look at the girl and assess her. Astonishingly like. But then he started thinking: was she wearing sandals? Or thongs, what the Brits (and Miriam) called flip-flops?

How treacherous memory is. You think you have noted everything, but as soon as you begin to go over the details you discover just how little you really did take in, after all.

Next time, he would make a point of being more precise, more specific in his observations.

If there was a next time.

But of course, the range of probabilities had been considerably strengthened, with this second sighting. It meant she was still in the area. More, it meant she was more likely to be in the specific Caloundra area, it eliminated all that long stretch of the Sunshine Coast, surely? It meant that from now on Charlie might keep his eyes open, might become more alert. It gave him some excuse to get out of the flat.

That already filled him with energy. Yes, it gave him a purpose.

+++++

The old codger was Bernie O'Connor and he had a little bait business over in Golden Beach. Charlie was sitting for the third morning in a row at the little café-bar on the road down towards the Passage. The young man who served him opened the conversation.

'Usual coffee this morning, sir? I note you got the usual earful from old Bernie yesterday, should have warned you but he's harmless, he's got this thing about foreigners, never sets a foot in this place, too modern for him, all this Italian coffee and the like. He still calls me wog boy but you get used to that, it's like me mother always going at me for saying fuckin' this fuckin' that, means nothing, now you'll have the raisin toast again this morning? or the crumpets? Or is it the bacon and eggs?'

Charlie beamed. 'You know how to make a person feel welcome.'

'That's my job sir. But it's the best job in Caloundra. I just love it. Get to meet everybody, and get to wear a smart outfit too. Well kinda smart. Not grunge, know what I mean? An outfit to be proud of.'

Charlie let him talk on, and then ventured a few observations about the scene since he had settled here. 'Strange how some things seem to remain fixed forever. There's still Henzell's Real Estate on the corner. Other things have been transformed. Who'd have imagined those weeping figs up the main street? Not everything's changed for the better, though.'

'Ah, living in Caloundra, is it? I'd put you down as a summer tourist only, sorry sir. Lots of them come up from the South to retire, but the summer usually knocks them about a bit, this place here has done a good turnover in preloved apartments as we like to say. What did you say your name was, sir?'

'Well, I haven't but it's Charlie Brosnan, and I picked up a very satisfactory three room flat over in Westaway Towers, so I'm not in the market for anything else, just in case you thought you might have a spotter's fee in mind.' He laughed, but made sure the young man hovered round a bit longer.

'It's a pleasure to hear a young person conscious of the way they dress. Must say, it suits you, too, the white shirt and black trousers.'

'If you want daggy, you get daggy. If you want class, I tell you in this place you can pick and choose.' He gave Charlie a bold wink, which left the older man momentarily puzzled but he nodded for another coffee.

When the waiter returned Charlie gave him a smile and sounded him out. This was virtually his first conversation all week and if anyone knew the possible lie of the land this confident young man was it.

'I suppose you get to know pretty well everyone around here, working at this place? What did you say your own name was, might I add?'

'Bronco, call me Bronco. Nobody calls me by my proper name.'

'Which is?'

The waiter's accent moved from flattened nasal diphthongs to fully rounded vowels and firm consonants. 'Umberto, Umberto Gioacchino Olivieri. Gioacchino is because of Gioacchino Rossini the composer, me dad was a nut for Italian opera.'

'Bravo. Where does your family come from, Umberto?'

'Bronco. A little place near Fiesole, but I'm third generation Aussie and proud of it. Me grandfather fell foul of the Fascisti, but my lot, we all speak Italian at home, just to make a point of it. My father says the Tuscan accent is the purest, have you heard the Venetian twang? Far out.'

Charlie, as he took a sip, looked at the young man more closely. There was something good-natured in his professionalism. Yes. He might be able to help.

'Caloundra has a fair passing trade then, d'you say? I guess you note all the talent? You know, the pretty girls?'

'Nothing moves in this village but I've got it tabbed, Mr ... er what did you say your name was'

'Brosnan. Charlie.'

'Right Charlie, sorry about that, usually pretty good, but you looking around for some pussy I can put you on to a few obliging ladies, friends of mine. Don't handle any of the jail-bait but. Gotta look after me good name and all that.'

Charlie was aware his polite smile had become more rigid. He put his dark glasses on, but then removed them. His eyes swivelled away from Bronco – from Umberto.

'No I was not digging for holiday sex, and, good Lord, you yourself said that in this town everybody knows everything about everyone, so I take your point on that. No, I was just wondering about a young lady I've seen these last couple of days. She looks stunningly like someone I knew some fifty years ago – long before your time, boy. I was wondering if she might be a relative or something. Of my old friend. It's funny, you know, coming back after all this time, suddenly to be reminded, to see this young girl like the spitting image ...'

But he paused there. Already he had given away too much.

Caution. Remember caution in unfamiliar contact. This place had a bizarre near-familiarity.

'Mate, you'll have to tell me more than that stuff about 'young lady' to give me some sort of clue. You're keeping it all in your mind. You know? All in your head, mate, none of it out in the open. What does she look like, this chick? Can you describe her for me?'

All in your mind. Yes, that was true. Charlie regretted how stupidly and willingly he had almost opened up to this smooth-faced gigolo with his crisp white shirt and his confiding voice. That one must hoard a treasury of gossip and blackmail, he must be like a fingerprint catalogue of the whole town. Already Charlie had spoken too much. Miriam had always said he was too gullible with strangers. She could be easily polite but distant. He was either too bottled-up or too prone to chatter, she had warned him.

He made the gestures of clearing his things from the small table. You couldn't be too standoffish or you'd discover nothing.

'The girl I saw was medium height, perhaps tall I guess, something your height in fact, and she has black hair, she's very pretty.'

Despite himself, he knew his voice conveyed a certain ardour. He rammed his hat on.

'Of course, dad. Sorry, Mr Brosnan. You've just described about every second lady in the whole area from Golden Beach to Noosa. You've got to be a bit more precise. What colour eyes? What sort of boobs?'

No need to feel proprietorial. No need to feel that his very thoughts were being fingered.

'Ah, well.' Charlie got up. He was aware of the young man looking at him, at his stiffening limbs. 'Next time I must take a note. If I see her again. She may have simply been down for the weekend.'

Bronco hovered attentively still and his smile was still broad, white toothed. Not threatening. Or possibly not.

'It was just an off chance. But she did remind me of someone I knew, all that time ago.'

Bronco moved Charlie's chair for him and began rattling crockery. 'See ya tomorrow then. Like to see someone make a habit of it. I can set the clock by old Bernie O'Connor. Down each morning, nine o'clock sharp. Never puts his nose into this joint, but. Thank God. Grumbling to himself half the time. But strict as clockwork, the old Bernie. I suppose routine is the big thing, your age?'

'Keeps you going,' Charlie replied curtly. He was not going to be completely bullied by this young oaf. Fiesole indeed! More likely the valley of the Po. Or even Calabria. He was almost swarthy enough. But not quite. Simply confident with the confidence of his own good looks and his youth and no doubt he turned the heads of every young visitor in town.

Do not become a grumpy old man. Do not.

Think of the ennui of a waiter's life. Especially here … the off season must be dullish, but perhaps Bronco went back to university to finish his Computer Graphics degree or his Business Management course. A name like that, he would play soccer like a devil, boasting of every move.

If Charlie were to become settled here, he must be prepared for the ups and downs.

There was no need to feel so possessive. Beatrice was hardly Charlie's private property. She had never been that. She had never been more than a childhood friend, no need to imagine at this stage anything more important.

But the image of Bronco hovering over her as she sat at one of the little metal tables, slyly noting her warm breasts, forcing her to smile back at him: no, he must not delude himself.

On his way up the hill he found himself looking out, turning his head, peering beyond shop windows into the darkened spaces within. Imagining possibilities.

Three

It was not so much a dream as something that came to him in that half waking, half somnolent state before dawn. It was a time when Charlie was, these days, restless and impatient with himself, half deciding to get up and half inclined to see if some sleep might return to release him for a couple more hours yet. Sometimes he turned on the radio, and listened to the five o'clock news, the six o'clock news, the seven o'clock. Sometimes he put on his headphones and listened to a CD. And this, often as not, worked: he woke up with his ears crushed and aching and no noise coming forth.

But this time, it was a month since he had begun to carve out a niche for himself in Caloundra and establish his patterns there, the images came more or less as a visitation. Yes, something out of the past, the early Caloundra past of course, but it was also something quite specific and intense in its reality for him. As if Charlie were still that adolescent boy with his blue jeans and his Hawaiian shirt feeling his oats and his possibilities. It was a nocturnal scene.

Curiously, he could not remember it. It had not been something that lodged in the memory bank and could be pulled out on whatever necessary occasion – looking over those old photographs, chatting with Alan about the old days, describing to his daughter the innocence of those holidays. His dream had been an unexpectedly vivid pageant of the mind, startling in its precision, utterly right but also utterly different. It was an evening over on the surf beach at the tip of Bribie Island.

A group of them, all teenagers. Dusk. They had been gathering a whole pile of driftwood from the wrack above the tideline. It had been piled to make a bonfire. As the shadow was pulled up from the east, over the waters, a grey-blue dustiness slowly colouring the whole sky, there was a sense of sudden urgency to get the job done and the fire actually started. That was the point at which the vision locked into precision. Charlie could feel his own combination of elation and anxiety as he dragged a particularly long, heavy log down from the dunes a couple of hundred yards south of the byre. He was calling out to the others to wait until he got it back there before they actually lit the whole shebang. He wanted to be in at the start of everything.

The night drops quite quickly in the sub-tropics. Ten minutes after the sun had set the beach was dark. The surf and the constant washes of fingering wavelets gave a sort of illumination, but now the fire had taken, and they were all sitting, on sandy blankets and towels, a safe distance from the flames. When the wigwam of the logs had collapsed into a glowing core, they would venture closer and begin their rough and ready sort of barbecue, with billy tea, potatoes in the embers and sausages stuck on twigs to be singed and blackened and then shoved between slices of bread and drenched with tomato sauce. There would be toast and a few of the braver souls had brought chops.

Someone regretted they had not thought to wrap a pig in banana leaves and place it under the fire to cook in its own juices. General cries of regret and envy.

No alcohol. He was certain of that; those were the years of truly simple pleasures. There were bottles of creaming soda and ginger ale and Helidon lemonade. It was not even the time of Coca Cola. Hot sweet tea out of the blackened billies was perhaps one of the unifying factors of the evening.

Some of the girls were shivering, they had not brought warm clothing, the afternoon had been so sunny and hot. But

on the beach suddenly chill airs were stirring and the excuse
to cuddle up together was irresistible. In groups, at first, they
found themselves huddled, with sauce on their hands and
the first rowdy round of popular songs already joining them
together jovially.

Jovial, that was the word. There was a sense of light-
hearted animation among them as a group. As the flames did
subside to the rich embers, someone would every now and
then wander into the darkness to search out another log or
piece of the pine planking that littered this immensely long
beach. The main traffic lanes ran parallel a mile or so out to
sea and there was always castoff jetsam here. Sometimes they
found the beach littered with hundreds of oranges, water-
logged and acid, or else pieces of rope and fishing buoys, some
of them made of limpet-encrusted glass. On this particular
evening, early, Charlie had brought back and presented to
Beatrice a pair of undamaged green glass buoys with their
rope netting still perfect and not encrusted.

Beatrice. Yes, she was there and, as the dream continued,
Charlie had his arm around her shoulders and she was snuggled in to him so that he sang more lustily and led the chorus
in the inevitable hoots of singing commercials from their
favourite radio shows. He got up and checked out the two
sausages-on-sticks that he had left to cook gently on the very
edges of the coals. He brought back two bakelite mugs of flat
lemonade. 'Tea will be ready soon,' he promised.

Yes, such innocence.

He was aware he was luxuriating in the small joyous-
ness of it. Surely in real life that evening had been full of as
many little irritations as of pleasures. Mosquitoes. Midges.
That chilly little wind off the water. Uncomfortable sandy
chafes in the groin. The tiny disappointment of half cooked
sausages.

No. The memory would have none of that. Everything
was blissfully happy and contentment more benign than such

ordinary human blemishes could spoil remained the pervasive quality of the whole experience. Charlie found himself smiling, and at that point he had to concede he had been dreaming of some illusion not some past reality.

Beatrice. Curious how she slid, again and again into his thoughts. It was as if the past somehow had not been able to accomplish its intent, as if life had taken a different course than that destiny, in some way, intended.

Alan had moved off to different associations, was it possible Alan even remembered Beatrice, after all these years? She had taken root in Charlie's consciousness, like some uncompleted act, some still unfinished business.

Charlie raised himself from the bed. All this was juvenile, he thought as he scrubbed his teeth, almost too vehemently. Fancy, after all these years, still even thinking of those lost moments. Was this what they described as 'being haunted?'

He had not been back to the little café on the front, by the Passage, not since that mawkish conversation with the young waiter.

Now he would have to exorcise in some other way this preoccupation with the charming angel of his youth.

+++++

Damn! He had allowed the milk to turn sour; how many days ago had he bought that carton? Never mind. Nothing for it but to get into his car and drive down for a replacement. While he was at it he might as well make it the little supermarket and stock up with whatever else was needed. Charlie felt he had become adept at household arrangements and he crouched down to see if potatoes, onions, tins of beetroot and Two Fruits needed topping up.

Already it was a hot morning. The holiday crowds had suddenly arrived, almost overnight the little town had become a bustling throng, and the most conspicuous addition to the sense of the changed environment was the presence of children. Children and young adults, in pairs and families. They were everywhere.

Instead of the usual quiet perambulation through the shelves of the supermarket, Charlie now felt he had to hurry. Somehow the zipping kids pushing their infant sisters in trolleys and the already overladen mums looking worried over the limp vegetables impacted on the atmosphere. He took out his list and quickly decided on the cold section first.

As he was reaching for his carton of milk he overheard a little group of young people talking in a noisy gabble and for some reason he turned round to inspect them. There, one of the two young women more or less in control of the party, almost within touching distance, was the girl herself.

Beatrice! He almost exclaimed it aloud, but stopped himself. Instead, he did raise himself up straight clutching his milk, and tried to catch her eye. She was too interested in the conversation going on around her to notice this white haired old man, with his red plastic basket and a one litre carton of milk in his hand.

'Excuse me', he said, too loudly. 'Excuse me, but there's something I wanted to ask you ...'

The other girl, closer to him, looked down. 'You can't reach the back shelf? Here, I can do that for you what is it you want – sliced cheese?'

'No, no' he said. 'I'm not ... it's not ... can you tell me your name?' He had caught her attention now, the right girl.

'Beg pardon? You speaking to me?' She had a fairly broad accent, though the vocal tone was musical, almost an echo. 'You're a bit cheeky for an old fella. Isn't he, Cassie'. But she relented, and was smiling (that smile! That smile!) 'Now why'd you want to go spoiling a perfect relationship by asking for personal details, mister? You young things just won't take no for an answer, but I tell you this. I don't go giving my name and address to just anybody, but you can

call me Trish if you want to. Now say thank you to Cassie
for getting you your soapy cheese and top o' the mornin' and
a Merry Christmas. You're not Santa himself, in an ocker
disguise, are you?'

And they went off together, arm in arm, with the silent
young men who had been standing behind them following
in their wake. Charlie heard their laughter still as he sheep-
ishly made towards the checkout, forgetting the remaining
items on his list. At the top of the tiny pile in the red basket
was a pack marked 'twelve easy-peel slices of Bodalla Tasty
Cheddar Cheese'.

He hadn't been rude, or improper in any way. He had not
consciously offended her. Why was she so anti-social then?
Why was she so antagonistic? Underneath the raillery of her
tone he had detected some hidden rancour. Was it directed
specifically at him? Or was it somehow more generalised?
Was she performing for the benefit of her friend – Cassie,
was it? –or for the silent youth lolling behind her, who had
said nothing, who had done nothing, who had simply strolled
along with the proprietary air of an Italian pimp.

No, Charlie was being altogether too offensive. There
was a streak of nastiness in him, he had to admit. It was as if
he were lumping all the young people together. Making it a
generational thing. Ridiculous!

And why hadn't he offered to explain? It would have been
straightforward. Direct and simple.

He had not even managed to get the name 'Beatrice' out.
That might have simplified everything. She would have seen,
by that name, there was someone she reminded him of, the
sort of thing that surely happens all the time, especially with
people around his age, nothing to be ashamed of in that. He
felt entirely ashamed.

By the time he reached his car, already over-hot in the
sun, that shame had turned to anger. Strangely, though, it
was directed to the first of the two young men, a person who

did not at all look like the driver of the white sports car the other week.

Swarthy.

Her name was Trish.

Altogether too great a leap of coincidence to think that could in any way be linked to a name like Beatrice. Patricia perhaps? And, looking at her more closely, as he had, it was clear there were other aspects of her features not at all like those he remembered.

The eyebrows, for instance. Beatrice had dark eyebrows, but surely thicker than that. These looked, well, plucked. He couldn't conceive of Beatrice ever considering such affectations; though he had not known her when she was a few years older, around the same age as this girl now.

And why be so aggressive?

He had done nothing to justify that.

It was her scorn, her absolute scorn. That had rankled.

+++++

'Charles! Charles Brosnan that is you? Over here,' and the plump lady with the blue rinse waved a chubby bare arm in his direction. Charlie had been sitting, finally, at the little coffee shop on Bulcock Beach, which he had decided he must return to. It was silly to allow himself to be – well – intimidated by some young thug in a white shirt and long black trousers.

Bronco, it turned out, was not on duty.

He looked up and saw her in her bright floral sundress and the large, rather elegant, straw hat. He could hardly miss her. She was nobody he could instantly recognise: certainly not someone out of his Melbourne past, in that rig-out. And hardly someone from his young Brisbane years. He would be unrecognisable.

'Charles Brosnan, fancy seeing you here of all places!' She had now got up and strode over, pulling out a seat for herself. 'I am right, aren't I? Now don't go telling me I've made another mistaken identity thing, no your very look tells me I'm right. But you don't have to look so stunned. It's Thelma. Thelma Jennings from two doors down.' And she laughed with genuine pleasure as Charlie, all too visibly, made the connection.

'I know I know. Seeing someone out of context, it happens all the time. But I knew it was you, I recognised Charles Brosnan the instant I set eyes. What are you doing here? Oooh. Oooh idiot me, of course. Poor dear Miriam, Charles I am sooo sorry, I meant to send a condolence but you know how things, and then we did Europe and the awful Trade Tower thing came and stranded us and, one thing and another, well we were relieved to be home and when Bruce said Noosa I said Darling so here we are. Except Bruce is talking investment things with someone at Henzells and Myra and me are left twiddling our cappuccino sugars.'

She hardly paused for breath. Charlie had pulled himself more upright and felt his spine straightening. The Woman From Next Door But One was a pain, but she and Miriam used to have a routine, when Miriam was at home, of having afternoon tea at the Moravia on Burke Road, they had been in the same Professional Women's Association at one stage. In living memory she had moved from fashionable black to dusty bruisey colours, but not yet, in Camberwell, to peacock.

'Now Charles, how about you? How are you keeping yourself? Are you looking after? I saw the house went up for sale and I had wonders but to see you all the way up here in sunny Queensland, it took the breath, but how ARE you?'

And for a moment he feared she would lean across and give him a pout on the cheek.

But she settled back in her chair and waved for her friend ('Myra') to come over. She was examining Charlie with paint-stripper eyes.

'Don't tell me. But why an out-of-the-way place like this? Unless you are a refugee from Noosa as well? You've got a home unit there. You've made a killing with real estate – just like my Bruce – and the views are marvellous aren't they, but the weather! My dear, it's a sauna! Still, when we go back to the saltmines we'll be brown as bandicoots. Or whatever.'

Charlie took a sip of his dead-cold coffee. 'You're right, it took me a moment to make the connection. Thelma Jennings of course. I really didn't expect to see you in a little place like Caloundra.' He didn't add that Caloundra had seemed a place where his past would not catch up with him. At least, that element of the recent past. 'I have a unit here, one of the older developments.'

'You're so wise. And I bet you offered peanuts. It's almost like taking lollies from kiddies, the prices up here. But there you go. And are you actually living here? Or is it your little retreat, your pied-à-terre? Myra, this is Charles Brosnan, our neighbour. Our FORMER neighbour.'

'How do you,' he muttered but he was already feeling hemmed in, indeed, genuinely uncomfortable, though he couldn't quite place why he should feel so antagonistic to Thelma Jennings who had actually been a shot in the arm for Miriam in that last year. She had jollied her along, got her out of herself, though Charlie did recall there had been some personal tragedy in her own life, that boy in Kew who kept on until he was almost twenty-one. Thelma had a way of bringing Miriam out of herself. Miriam, who in the past had never been a one to dwell. No, he had a lot to thank Thelma for, and he must not remain grumpy.

'Myra, Charles has just joined the legion of sun-seekers, he's nosed out a unit here for almost nothing. We're thinking of a pad somewhere around Southbank ourselves, have you considered that, or have you made a similar killing already? He's such a quiet one, Myra. Still waters run deep, I always said that to Miriam. But, oh Charles I am sorry, I did not mean to come barging in on you dwelling on your loss and poor Miriam. We do miss her, miss her dreadfully actually, but now it's time to keep on living and I applaud you, Charles, I envy you for your strength in making a big move like this. I never in all the years that I knew her heard Miriam even mention Queensland or the Sunshine Coast so it must be a really big thing for you, Charles, this move, getting away from ... well, everything. All those memories.'

'Queensland is where I grew up. I spent my youth. Or at least, until I was eighteen. So it has been a sort of return. Not an escape.'

'Some things we just have to escape, I understand that Charles, but that's not the word I would use. After someone, well special, like Miriam, I can understand the need to make a break. Make a break. Well, that almost sounds more direful than 'escape' doesn't it? What is the word I am seeking? Come on Charles, you're the Scrabble champion, what is the word I am seeking?'

'I think I would say I have come to Caloundra to renew myself, Thelma. Does that seem to you ruthless? I think Miriam would understand it. It is not running away from, more a shuffling towards. At my age you don't run, if you can help it.' And he laughed, sealing off the conversation and the increasing closeness of her antennae, in a way that left only a polite retreat possible. There were excuses, vague indications toward watches, and no invitation for a further round of coffee.

'I am keeping you, Charles. Miriam always forgave you your habit of looking at your watch, did you know that? My husband, she said, my husband lives by the clock, whereas I live by the moment as it comes. She was a wonderful person, your wife. But of course you know that. She tolerated so much. Even me, but I knew I released the girl in her, and what a wonderful girl that was. Do you know, just one month before she flew off to that Greek conference – we didn't know, we didn't dream – we had coffee in the Moravia and she said to me, 'It's Charlie I worry over, since he retired. I have to find him routines to follow. We play chess and Scrabble on alternate nights, that sort of thing.' And all the time it was Miriam who was … but I must not go on, it is too sad, it is all too sad.' And she dismissed him with her lipstick curved into a huge smile, or a wreath.

Had he ever really known Thelma? He had encountered her often enough, in a hallway and vestibule sort of way. A truly horrifying thought insisted itself – had he ever known Miriam? Of course he had known HIS Miriam, but Thelma seemed to be speaking of another person altogether. One can only cling to one's own explanation.

As he walked, briskly he hoped, towards the foreshore path and away from the town centre, he saw the old curmudgeon (What was his name? O'Connor?) sitting at that park bench, as if he had never left it. Was it a month already? He was dressed in identical rags. It was almost pitiful, really. But Charlie recalled the vehemence and bigotry in the old boy's voice, and the figure transformed itself into an image of stubborn insult.

Rigid and impossible. God forbid that Charlie would ever devolve to that! The horror was: for the first time he recognised a sort of possibility.

He veered away. But he knew if he were to live here he had to come, somehow, to terms with the locals, the regulars. He could have found plenty of old bigots like O'Connor around Melbourne, he had only to scratch the surface. But it had been possible, there, to carve out your own life, your own friends, even the suburb congenial to you. Everything was compressed up here. Close at hand. Inescapable.

The last time he had walked this particular way back towards Westaway Towers, the weather had been noticeably cooler. Now it was oppressively sultry. He felt the sweat trickle down his back, before his shirt stuck. He was aware of the dark stains under his arms and the body odour, even though he had showered before he went out this morning.

This morning. The supermarket and that encounter seemed now something distant, remote.

Thelma Jennings had caught him by surprise, she had caught him out. But she had also taken his mind from the preoccupation that had been becoming a sort of idealised fantasy, of that young woman reminding him of Beatrice, a fantasy that somehow had tricked him into dreaming of all those decades back, of himself as a burgeoning young sprig.

Thelma in that sense brought him into context. Miriam was not to be exorcised, nor should she be. Miriam was herself, her magnetic self. Thelma had been certainly wrong: it was not a running away at all; hadn't he in his mind still shared so many things with Miriam, almost unconsciously, like the way he kept to the routine of that Bushells Espresso, or her preferred breads. Even the selection of TV channels echoed Miriam's preference, and indeed, as he had to admit to himself, the hollow feeling of not being able to share the game of Scrabble while they watched *The Bill*. The shadow of Miriam was still there, all right.

They had developed a routine, certainly, but it was an affirming thing.

He must not allow himself to become tetchy like this.

And he must not allow himself to return to chafing over that silly incident in the supermarket this morning. No point. No point in feeling angry at that perfectly innocent and self-centred young woman. No point in feeling angry with himself. What's over is over. We always think of the clever reply twenty minutes after the confrontation or the irksome encounter. No point, any more, and particularly no point in willing it all back again, to brood over and to lick, like an old sore. How ridiculous.

Thelma Jennings. What Miriam always enjoyed about Thelma was her ebullience, she was the world's most unself-conscious extrovert.

But when she had first hailed him, waving that large fleshy hand and shaking her thick coloured mass of hair, he knew what had been his first, surprised, thought.

'Is that Beatrice? Beatrice in her maturity, the Beatrice who was the same age, the same generation as myself, old Charlie?

+++++

He had automatically wandered on from the end of the promenade, through the lightly timbered picnic area and then through a little break in the retaining fence onto the beach itself. It was at the point where the Stillwater of the Passage swept over towards the tip of Bribie Island and formed a wide bank, the other side of which was surf.

He was tempted to take off his shoes, but then decided otherwise and stomped gingerly through the soft sand until he came to a groin of black volcanic stones and here he did give up on the thought of trudging much further so he clambered up a set of rough stairs and found himself at a turnaround for vehicles; bitumen and the first clustering sets of low-rise units. A sign said Dingle Avenue and he knew this led uphill to the ridge and, in a little way, his set of apartments.

The climb was steeper than he realised and he found himself puffing and looking stolidly at the ground in front of him as he pushed himself, foot by foot, up the steep grade, keeping mainly to the grassy sward rather than the road.

Which was why, as he came to a pause at the higher ring-around, he was so surprised when he almost bumped into the little group striding down from the shops. Beatrice was among them.

'Excuse us, sir,' one of them jumped aside, onto the road, to avoid a collision. 'Oh, it's him. It's your admirer, Trish!' And they all laughed and waved to Charlie as they bounced around him, leaving him stranded.

She had gone on with them, and he could distinguish her laughter from all the others. She did not look back.

Still breathing heavily, eventually he continued his trek uphill, the last leg of that climb. He was thinking nothing, nothing. He was concentrating on his climb, one foot after the other, counting the number of steps now, as if that might somehow ease the distance.

Those young people. As if they owned the footpath, the whole street and no doubt they would be sprawling out on the sand shortly, littering it with their presence and their papers and plastic castaways and their towels and beach umbrellas and whatever else made them territorial.

She had seen him. She had recognised him. She had ignored him.

That was the order of things, of course it was and it would remain that way. Until he could get the opportunity – privately, he now realised, without her cohorts urging her on to adopt that defensive, yes defensive, stance.

The question was so simple, merely to satisfy himself that the amazing coincidence between this girl and Beatrice would be explained by some genetic inheritance. She would be curious, and probably slightly excited at the accident, and might be able to tell him about her grandmother (he had convinced himself it must be that) and where she lived, what she had done in her life, where she had finally settled.

When he did reach the top of the incline, instead of taking the easy gradient on to his building, Charlie made a quick decision. He was glad he had worn his sun hat. It was sticky and oppressive now, approaching 11.30. He went downhill again. He made his long away to the approaches of Kings Beach. He guessed already that the little group would not head right for the main surfing area with the lifesavers' hut and the green parkland, nor up to the rocks and the artificial rock pool. They would have erected their shade among the further dunes, back toward the Passage a bit. More privacy.

He was right. He congratulated himself on his acuity, but remembered, of course, that back in the old days they themselves had sometimes chosen that section, though back then nobody would have dared to sunbake topless.

For a minute or two he stood, leaning his hand on a splintery fencepost dividing off the dunes from the encroaching flats. These had not been here before. But he caught sight of Beatrice running back from the surf with one of the young men. She beat him, and threw herself down on the sand near a blue and red umbrella and then with a towel she vigorously mopped her hair and under her arms. Charlie watched every move.

They were not twenty yards away, perhaps less. After a while the others went back into the water but Beatrice remained. After a few minutes, without bothering to look round to scrutinise the dunes she undid the top of her bikini. She lay with her face in the shade of the umbrella and the rest of her out in the open.

Charlie did not move. Initially he had determined that this was the moment to go up to her and ask his simple question. But once he saw that she had armed herself with that exposure he hesitated. He did not want to be thought a voyeur. He remained where he was. He mopped his face. He adjusted his spectacles. He was sweating.

How long he remained like that was not the question, time in a sense had been stilled. But he was suddenly and abruptly grabbed on the shoulder. With a wrench that nearly unbalanced him he was twisted round.

'Bloody old pervert!' The young man had sprung over the little retaining fence and, wearing only swimming gear, his muscles were conspicuous and tensed. 'You miserable old bastard, get right outa here or I'll get the cops. Or the Beach Inspector.' He shoved Charlie backwards without releasing his grip. 'Or, better still, some of the blokes at the Lifesavers, they'll teach you a lesson!'

It was the young man of the white sports car. He was carrying in one hand two ice-cream buckets. His other hand still like a vice upon Charlie's shoulder, he shook him with each word.

'I saw you. All the way back from the kiosk I was watching you perving on her.' He gave Charlie another shove so that he almost unbalanced. 'I know it was Trish you were perving, you've been sniffing around her for ages now, don't think I haven't seen you.' He released his grip and the older man shuffled involuntarily to regain his footing, aware that this gave him a further disadvantage. 'What do you think you're up to, an old man like you? You should be ashamed.'

He was looking at Charlie more closely, with more quiz-zical curiosity, rather than anger. The ice cream buckets were clearly melting and he made as if to move onto the dunes toward the umbrella.

'You've got me wrong,' Charlie finally exclaimed, and his voice sounded strangely high and broken, as if he had a frog in his throat. He grunted, and then began again, this time pitching his words from the lower register.

'Do you think at my age I want to ogle young women? I'm a grandfather myself, godsake, I was just waiting until she got herself dressed a bit more respectably ...'

'Bloody hypocrite, that's what you are! I saw you, I tell you. Not only here on the beach this morning. Or at the super-market earlier on, don't think we didn't see you the other day, sneaking after us into the pictures, and the day before that, further along this very beach, when we were surfing and sun-baking, don't think we didn't all see you sitting in your car and perving, stood out like a beacon.'

'I wasn't on the beach.'

'Wearing those reflector sunglasses; couldn't get enough from the car, you walked right out onto the beach, with your shoes and socks, looking like a bloody South Right Whale, drooling over all the nice young flesh.'

'That wasn't me.'

'Everyone on the beach saw you, not that you took any notice, perving and drooling.'

'One moment. Look, that girl reminds me of ...'

'Your granddaughter, oh yes, all of that, tell me another.' The young man cast a glance at the sodden containers, and began to stride onto the sand dune, but he called out, 'Just clear out or I really will lose my temper and it will be more than soggy ice cream I shove into your face and rub it in.'

'I once knew somebody ...'

'Off!'

'Somebody she reminds me of ...'

'OK. That's it. Here, you come along with me and we'll soon sort this out.'

'Very well, I will leave. But ask your friend if she is related to someone who was once called Beatrice Linton ...'

'Never heard of her, and Trish is my sister. Now move! Move, I tell you.'

But the young girl herself had come over, her bikini top now adjusted. Charlie had not noticed as she came up behind him.

'Peter, what on earth is it? Oh, my ice cream! Peter, you've let it all melt! Oh!'

Then her voice changed. 'Oh, it's you again.'

She looked Charlie up and down quite frankly, her face screwing up with distaste. How could he possibly ask her the question now?

'This your grandpa, Trish? That's what he claims he is.' And the young man gave loud chortle as he passed over the bucket. 'Sorry about the ice cream. Come on, another.' He put his arm around her waist. 'Beatrice Linton, that's the name he said, you heard of a Beatrice Linton?'

'Peter don't be silly. Isn't this ... aren't you the old man we helped this morning, over at the supermarket?'

Charlie nodded but his opportunity was lost. 'You look like someone ...'

'Off, I said. Leave the lady alone.' Peter now assumed genuine command and moved back to Charlie and gave him a shove on the chest. 'And don't keep tailing us around like you have been. You're a marked man, know that? We've got you tabbed. Did I tell you, Trish, I saw him down at the picnic grounds on Bulcock Beach two or three weeks back, talking to your uncle Bernard? He's been hanging around like a bad smell.'

'Really? Look, old man, I don't like being followed. Everywhere I go, everything I do. Especially if Uncle Bernie is around ...'

'This is ridiculous. I only wanted to catch you because you look so remarkably like ...'

'Someone's granddaughter. That gives you no excuse to stand perving on my girlfriend while she is tanning herself.'

'I thought you said ...'

'Off! I mean it this time. Off.'

'You're not the one Peter said had been sitting with binoculars up the beach there wetting himself to perve on all the girls? That's disgusting.'

'That was not me. This is the first time I have even come onto this beach.'

'I've seen him everywhere. After that first time, I've kept an eye out, we don't like people like you hanging around taking advantage.'

'Just let him go, Peter. I'll come up with you for that ice cream, this one's ruined.' And she threw it without a thought over the crest of the dune, among marram grass, and dragged him away. As they went off she said to Peter, 'My grandmother? Can you believe it, Grannie's a hundred and the only thing Grannie looks like is the Simpson Desert! And Grannie lives in Gladstone anyway.'

Charlie was already back on bitumen. His face was flushed and he found himself erratic, he had to hold onto things. From here the route back to his flat was steeply uphill.

+++++

Anger is a complicated process, it finds its target but the target moves and becomes displaced, or it stays rigid while your feelings swirl like tides through the narrow channel, scouring a new passage and churning up everything in its way, cutting and distorting while at the same time seemingly intent on absolute directness.

Charlie took a long time to cool down. His apartment was like a prison and for the first time he felt the invisible bars. He paced the length of it, from the back bedroom past the two other bedrooms, none of them used, out to the living area and to the kitchen as if food or refrigeration might deflect some of his turbulence.

A dozen times he must have done this before he pulled himself up. He was drenched. He ripped off his clothes and marched to the shower.

He dabbed himself dry and strode to the bedroom to find himself something. Everything he looked at seemed to have the sly look of old men who sat with binoculars behind the wheels of expensive cars and studied the nubile young bodies so flagrantly conspicuous everywhere.

They flaunt themselves on purpose!

But he corrected himself. He found a plain white shirt, remnant of the Melbourne years.

There was enough food in the place to last several days. He felt a huge reluctance to go outside.

At a certain stage he conceded that the young man, Peter, was probably acting nobly, protectively. It was simply that he was utterly wrong. And Charlie realised that there was no way he could prove that. These things do not depend upon facts, they depend upon feelings.

The anger became self-directed, then it became surly and Peter, Trish, everyone he could think of became his enemies. And of course, inevitably, he began to question why he had come to Caloundra, this haunted place, as a way of remaking his life.

'You don't have to take it lying down. Where's that old canniness ...?' His own words seemed to sneer back at him. What was the alternative? Melbourne? Hadn't he gone to all the effort of cleaning out everything there? He couldn't go back. He just had to be patient. He could not afford to upset himself over trifles. Think of it that way: trifles.

Two days.

Finally, he had to make the decision: This was ridiculous! Why allow himself to be bullied in this way? He found his sun hat and decided to walk down to the village. He had not even bought his regular newspaper. He would, almost defiantly, have a coffee and croissant in the little café where he had started to become a regular.

He paused in the foyer and then reached for his car keys. He drove down.

And it did feel better, getting out and about. The young Italian waiter was not there. Why should that be a sort of relief? Bronco had been no threat – he had even shown a willingness to help. It was Charlie's own fault that he had felt rubbed up the wrong way. Young people were all like that. It was not Bronco particularly. All of them.

Charlie was served by a middle-aged soul with vivid red hair and sagging, freckly skin, a sure candidate for skin cancer, he thought. He vaguely recalled her at other tables. Not appealing. But he had his coffee and even the croissant,

greasy with butter and thawed, flaky pastry which nevertheless seemed rubbery. Raisin toast was no longer a possibility.

He looked around. There, down the end of the street, was
the picnic table where he had encountered Bernie O'Connor.

The girl, Trish, could not possibly be related to that redneck old bully, surely? Look at him there, arrogant and proprietorial, shoving his jaundiced views down the craws of
everybody in hearing distance. Her Uncle? And of course he
had to admit such a thing could be possible.

Uncle Bernie O'Connor? The old man was dressed in his
habitual gear and, sure enough he had a small crowd of young
people around him. He was holding forth so loudly Charlie
could catch some of the exclamations from here. The listeners
were laughing and it almost seemed they were good-heart-
edly teasing him. Urging him, rather. For just one second
Charlie felt a surge of protective annoyance at them, the
young baiting the old, but it passed. Perhaps they had a better
technique to defuse the old man's assertiveness? Perhaps they
were not really listening at all, merely indulging him, making
him a toy to their all too self-confident superiority.

He was so engrossed in the spectacle – there were three
young women, all with large straw hats and protective
long sleeves –that he let his coffee grow cold. As he turned
round to catch the eye of the waitress he saw, standing quite
close behind him, the muscular young man, Peter. He was
glowering.

There was a pause. Both seemed taken aback, Charlie at
being so blatantly the subject of such intent gaze; Peter at
being caught out before he had worked out his tactics.

'I'm watching. I'm keeping an eye on you,' Peter said, in a
hoarse whisper, as he picked up his knapsack from between
his feet and walked down the concrete verge, past Charlie
and towards the end of the street.

'Don't you threaten me,' said Charlie before he so much as
thought. 'I have a perfect right …'

'What's that?' Peter turned round and took a pace back. 'What's that you say? You're the one needs to understand what threatening means. You're a stalker. And I've got my eyes on you. Don't think you can stalk Trish, or anybody else for that matter. You don't stalk people round here with impunity.' He swung the haversack as if it would make a useful weapon. 'You're being watched, Stalker. You understand that? You're being watched every time you poke your nose outside the Westaway Towers.'

Even his home was tagged? Charlie half rose, but sensibly decided on silence. He had his rights. He did not have to quarrel with some young thug about those. If necessary, he would go to the police himself, lay a complaint.

The young man had marched off, shoulders almost pathetically straight so that Charlie was reminded of Young British Chaps of Impossible Virtue. Except that this young man had a broad accent and the matter of virtue was probably something he didn't even understand. He had lied before. He had dented his own credibility pretty powerfully, then. He had … but there was no point in pursuing the subject, all the self-justifying speeches counted for nothing, in the event.

As he gathered up his newspaper and his hat, Charlie did look down towards the Front. The virtuous Peter was standing, one foot on one of the park benches, and with his hand on the shoulder of one of the young women listening to the monologue of that old bigot O'Connor. Just as he looked more closely at her she took off the hat. Beatrice. Trish. Whoever.

It was the first time for two days that the name 'Beatrice', in its specific resonance, had crossed his mind. It had been displaced so that 'Trish' now occupied that territory where once so much sweet and painful memory had gathered itself. Trish, who threw ice cream containers thoughtlessly onto the sandhill and who laughed, he recalled, with a sort of implicit spite and carelessness that belonged to herself entirely, of that he was certain. More than certain. Oh yes. The niece.

It was not exorcism. But it was the tatters of anger, without regret or conditions. Anger, even in its dregs, carries its own sense of virtue about it. It is the most untrustworthy of passions.

+++++

To get to his car he would have to walk down to Bulcock Street and pass that little coven of witches and wizards. They looked settled for a long sitting, from the way their laughter and joking continued. Charlie tried to prevent himself, but he was pretty sure he was in their firing line, as well as any passing refugees or non-Irish strangers.

This was impossible. He couldn't allow himself to be tyranised by nonsense of that sort. But he did not move. He ordered another coffee.

These standover tactics were Hollywood movie, not normal Caloundra laissez-faire and goodwill. Oh, if they really thought he had been stalking, it was the sort of thing that had been in the news down in Melbourne only recently, yes he could understand a sort of rancour, but what he had done was entirely innocent, it was ridiculous to compare it with that sort of business. Though what really rankled was the realisation that she clearly had no intention of letting him approach her again. Not to mention her watchdog, that Peter. He had to relinquish the thought of ever uncovering the mystery and coincidence of her uncanny resemblance. Though, as he had been realising more and more clearly, this Trish, close up, was not at all like Beatrice, not the voice, not the texture of her skin, not the real colour of her eyes. It was just a more general sense of shape, of hair – that still uncannily reminded him of her – the youthful bounciness of her body in action. Even the way Trish had grabbed at Peter's arm as they raced off to the kiosk, that had echoes. But they now had become ironic, almost parodies.

He thought once more of the way Trish had tossed that ice cream container. Something about it both irritated him, and intrigued him. It was like an echo of something forgotten. Had Beatrice ever done something like that, on the beach, up along the dunes? In those days they were pretty careless about littering. No. Nothing he could recall.

His second coffee was finished and out of the corner of his eye he noticed that the picnic bench was now empty. Thank God. Was he to spend the rest of his life skirting and evading? No way.

He reached for his belongings and eased himself of the metal chair. Halfway down the footpath he was hailed loudly by that Camberwell woman, Thelma Jennings. She was still here.

'Charles Brosnan, over here. Yoo Hoo. I'm so glad I caught up with you again Charles. I have been coming down to this café with its dreadful coffee and absolutely despicable croissants every day just in the hope of seeing you. Look. Look what I've got, I had to hand it to you I knew you would be thrilled.' And she scrabbled amongst the things in her capacious purse and drew out a coloured photograph, studio size. It was of Miriam and herself, in some rather grand function judging by the table decorations. They were hugging each other and both of them laughing boisterously.

'See! That's me, in my Thai silk. Miriam always said she envied me that. And isn't Miriam so gorgeous? Simply gorgeous! Miriam was a star. But of course you know it. You knew it. Look, I've had a copy so you can keep this one. I just thought you must have it. It is the best one of Miriam, of both of us. Here, I'll wrap it in a Kleenex so it doesn't get smeared. Now go, run off, my duty is done, promise delivered. I am not going to detain you, I know you are busy. And after our meeting the other week, well I was weepy all afternoon, and that does nothing for my skin texture I can tell you. A big kiss and a hug, then? Ah, Charles, Charlie. Now go.'

In the hot inner bubble of his car Charlie did study the photograph.

Everything had become activated by hidden trip wires. The Miriam in the photograph was at most a stranger. She was a Miriam from another life. A Miriam with another life. The self seemed to stretch endlessly

When Miriam smiled for the camera with Charlie, she always took off her glasses and composed her features, it was a habit. Here, her spectacles made a sort of mask of her face. Except this mask wore a different expression. Unburdened. No, that was not the word. He looked at it again, and then carefully placed it in the seat beside himself, and drove off.

Westaway Towers was the only place to return to.

When he opened the door he was looking into a tomb.

+++++

There are routines to keep you busy. Why be ashamed of that?

He had considered taking the *Australian* down to some shady spot, though not in the O'Connor territory. Now he found himself back in his flat, with the glossy photograph of Miriam demanding careful handling, no salt or sand thank you. It had lost its initial affront. He placed it flat on the neat dining table next to his paper, and once he had made himself the requisite coffee (yet another! He would have to watch it) he opened the paper out and began browsing in his usual headline-skimming way.

Miriam would quiz him when she emerged, bleary eyed: 'What news today? What are the main reports?' He could usually parrot the banners but Miriam, that relentless reader of full reports, was never satisfied. She remembered the names of even remote political figures, be it some Egyptian

Foreign Minister or the Head of the Army in Pakistan ('He is also their Prime Minister') and Charlie's vagueness once it got to details infuriated Miriam. 'You neglect to get the names right. Names are important.'

Names have no importance. None whatsoever. That is something he had only recently discovered, and with some pain.

He turned the first page, then stopped. He folded it back and conscientiously read every word of all the lead articles. The photograph merely revealed Miriam's public, extrovert smile, so wholehearted. Nothing else. That quality seemed painful now, it was the necessary quality Charlie knew he lacked. The paper hardly seemed worth reading, without the thought of Miriam there to report to. The photograph became, increasingly, an entire mask. Who might know what lies behind the mask? What lay behind?

He tossed the paper away from him. He picked up the photograph and was surprised that the anger was so palpable. It was not against Miriam. It was something within himself.

This was all becoming impossible. He picked up his car keys and headed out once again. This time, after cruising with a sort of aimlessness round and round the main streets of the compact village, he found a parking spot. It was outside the chemist so he went in. Looking around, he picked up a pair of wraparound sunglasses, very dark. He tried them on. The perfect disguise. Then he skimmed through the adjacent rack of sun hats. Chemists these days sell everything. He took one of those deplorable things called, he thinks, golf caps. He tried it on also. Utterly non-Charles Brosnan, it made him look like some tennis clone. He bought them both and then, to complete the picture, he added a pair of black thongs, the sort of thing Miriam abhors. Abhorred. He, also. He walked out with a sense of grim satisfaction.

Wait. Something else caught his eye as he was leaving the Pharmacy. A pair of binoculars. That, too.

With a fierce pleasure he threw them onto the front seat and drove off, rather too abruptly so that a woman with her whole week's groceries looked as if he intended to skittle her. 'Sorry!' he called out loudly, giving her a wave but not stopping.

He found himself, almost without thought, down on the flat along King's Beach. It was near where the incident with Peter happened yesterday at around this time. He found a place to park the car, closer to the main surfing area. He sat for several minutes, casing out the joint. He laboriously took off his shoes and then the long grey socks which had become his uniform up here, if he were not wearing full length trousers. His feet looked white, exposed. The black thongs increased this sense of nakedness.

He was wearing the very dark glasses. The cap was in place. He dragged himself out of the front seat and walked towards the sand. The area was crowded with sunbathers and families under beach umbrellas or other shelter. He walked among them, for the first time feeling hidden by his new camouflage. He selected a hillock of sand, loosely strewn with marram grass, and took a long, steady look.

From this position he could get a sense of the total beach area. On the northern side, quite close, the basalt rocks and the artificial rock pool were crowded with kids. A few pandanus palms that he remembered from old times still seemed to have grown not at all in the intervening fifty years. He looked in the southern direction. It was along there a little way that Beatrice – Trish – had taken off her bikini top. He stood up to get a better view.

As he did so he noticed a young man – a lad merely – who was sprawled out in a dip in the sand. He was asleep. But his body had betrayed him. A strong erection had lifted the front of his Speedo trunks with obvious results. Charlie moved off, feeling indignant. Why? Nobody else seemed even to have noticed. It is almost as if he, himself, were complicit.

Everywhere he looked, a sort of carnal energy pervading

everything. Even asleep, we are betrayed by it. And we are betrayed by the hidden excitements that are part of the body.

Admit it. There is a trace of the voyeur in everybody.

He had not noticed, before, that set of home units almost right on the sand, towering above this section of the beach. What sort of council regulations have been flaunted, who has been bribed, to secure such a frontage? It is surely not only illegal but downright dangerous, should a cyclone come sweeping along this coast, not at all an unlikely prospect.

He pulled out his new binoculars from their case, already sand-smudged. His first practical application of their use was to scrutinise those units. On the third floor one balcony had a gaudy sign. No doubt TO LET and probably with the additional information HOLIDAY VACANCY. Rates doubled or trebled for the Christmas rush, it must be at a particularly high rental not to be snapped up already. He noted the name of the agent, Ray White Caloundra.

On the beach below those units he saw another group of young people – teenage girls, squirming almost out of their costumes. Animated, so unconsciously sexual.

This is madness. Replacing the binoculars, Charlie already knew what was required of him. His anger had been converted into a sort of excitement. One week. Only one week, but think of the possibilities. Quite apart from the sense of the hunter and the quarry, there was the feeling of liberation, of intent. There was also the sense that he had outwitted that musclebound oaf Peter. And, when he finally admitted it, there was the sense of opportunity. He would be able to gaze, unhindered, for as long as he liked upon the youthful nudity of Trish or whoever, and nobody would interrupt him, he would be safe, legally, on his own private territory, at least for one week, and they could do nothing about it.

All the furies that have been seething within him are replaced by some sort of chemical process into this excitement, this location, this eagerness.

+++++

Before he returned to Westaway Towers the deed was done. He is quite animated and only now half admits to himself what a hairbrained plan this is. Yes, it might be hairbrained but it is also strangely releasing. He feels in power again, in command. The object is almost only a secondary consideration; he keeps deferring the delicate pleasure he has set in store for himself, almost as if that were not the real consideration. He will be able to soak into that all in good time.

One week rental, a truly ridiculous rental and an even more spectacular deposit but things like that are not the point, they are the necessary hurdles. He gets the key tomorrow at 10 a.m.

There is the rest of the day to fill in. Charlie takes his car out again, there is a restlessness that now has a proper focus. He feels not only safe behind his new dark glasses but also invulnerable. So this is why disguises are so irresistible? He had sometimes ragged Miriam about her cosmetics, her 'disguises' he had called them. 'You don't need all that make-up, you are wonderful just the way you are,' he had always said, and meant it. Her tolerant smile had become one of their little secret exchanges.

+++++

Where to? After a few minutes thought Charlie decided to drive over to Dicky Beach, where the ancient wreck still protruded out of the sand, or at least he imagined it did. It was a quieter beach, less popular with children and family groups because the surf there was rather more treacherous, sudden rips and dragging tides. At Moffatt Beach, just along the way, a small creek crossed the sand and that had always been a popular children's play area.

Dicky Beach was, as he anticipated, only inhabited by a

scatter of people. The weather had turned overcast, which probably made the sand less attractive, and the surf looked positively treacherous. He walked some distance in his chafing thongs and the golf cap. He carried only the binocular case over his shoulder, no towel, no other accessories.

Pushing through the sand roused old, adolescent memories, even impulses. He ran a few paces, then paused and caught his breath. He was almost inclined to yodel into the wind, which dried his lips with a salty tang. How long since he had felt this sort of eagerness? This silly anticipation?

He saw them, half hidden in the high dunes, only when he was almost on top of them. A group of half a dozen. They were all completely naked, the men as well as the women. Charlie paused.

Too late. He had been sighted.

The three young men sprang up and in a rush were upon him, faces made ugly with threat and vehemence. Creatures in their prime, Charlie thought, even as they came upon him and surrounded him.

'It's him again!' Peter shouted, 'It's the Stalker!' And they had him by the arms, the shoulders, before he could begin to think such things as self-defence.

'He deserves the lot!'

'He should be knackered, I'll get my Swiss Army knife.'

'No way. Might give the girls ideas!' And they shouted their laughter over him, ignoring his own voice, concerned only with heaving him bodily towards the brown-tinged surf.

He could not see what the girls were doing. Had they remained on the dunes? Laughing and jeering? Were they perhaps even frightened? He was roughly shoved and dragged over the sand. He lost one thong. He began shouting. He did not realise there was such indignation in him. Such anger.

They carried him out to the surf, despite his protests. They were laughing and jostling him now. There was also the hard thump at his kidneys and the tearing off of his spectacles. He was clutching the binocular case but that was not their interest. They had surged right out into the swirl of surf so that the first big wave broke over them and they ducked and spluttered but still gripped him hard. It was only in very recent times that Charlie had become aware how his skin had lost its pliability, it broke too easily, it bruised and gave him visible marks with almost any pressure.

Like a sack they dragged him further out into the salty surf. Like a bundle of rubbish, an old car tyre. He could not move his arms.

These youths were treating his body like plastic. He shouted out and protested. He threatened, but they ignored him completely.

'Right out,' one of them said. It was horseplay and he would have to endure it, there were no nearby witnesses, it was a change room gang up. He gave up his efforts.

A further spill of surf engulfed them all, they were ducked underneath, but none of them let go. Charlie felt himself being pushed underwater. He struggled now, more vehemently. He felt his arms straining to get free. The binocular case was no longer clutched to his chest, he was struggling with panic now to find air, to break surface.

Drowning was not possible. He had not considered drowning. Water and sand abraded his face, his eyes. It was not possible. It was not possible. When you lose balance you lose everything. The pressure was from above. They were drowning him.

He must have fainted. There was no recollection of them releasing their brutal grip, no sense of how or when he had been released. He found himself half-in half-out of the tide-line, in a mess of smelly seaweed. It was a minute before he could open his eyes properly, and his throat felt scalded. Nobody came to his rescue.

He did not know how long. He only knew he had not swallowed anything. His mouth had remained clasped. They had not beaten him. They had beaten him thoroughly with the carelessness of youth, with impunity. The stiffness was beginning.

Two seagulls poked towards him on the sand. They skirted him and continued prodding and pecking. He half-rose, finally, and then sank back. Another weak surge of wave half-lifted him up but that was all.

When thought returned, he would be ropeable. Not yet.

+++++

He spent some while, later, searching for the binoculars. He did find one black thong. His clothing was still drenched and by now it was chafing him. The skin of his body felt as if rasped by sandpaper.

They were nowhere in sight. Did he expect they would be?

When he finally trudged back to the car his first, sudden, thought was: car keys? They were still attached by the little clip to his belt. At least that humiliation was avoided.

When he did reach the vehicle, however, it took him a few moments, after starting the motor, to realise what was wrong.

All four tyres had been flattened and the air valves were missing.

It took him quite a while before he worked out that the next thing to do was to phone the RACQ.

While awaiting their arrival he felt for his wallet. It, fortunately, was also still there, perhaps miraculously, all things considered.

He must be starting to feel better, to be able to feel relieved over that.

Inside, with his money (how fortunate that the new plastic currency seemed unsoakable) was also a very sodden piece of paper. It was the receipt from Ray White Caloundra for one week's rental of the third floor home unit on Kings Beach.

That was when, finally, he vomited.

+++++

Miriam had raced ahead into the surf. Her naked flanks pale in the hot sun but she turned and urged him on. Charlie, on the edge, clumsily balanced from foot to foot as he dragged his underpants off. The long beach was empty, except for the thread of seawrack so typical of Bribie Island. When he caught up with her they sprayed each other and laughed till he embraced her and they flopped down in the shallow water, gasping. Another roller loomed over them and they were dunked. He grabbed her arm and held for dear life as he felt her being dragged from him. Later, he realised that there were dangerous rips along that part of the coast. Anything might have happened.

To wake in the night, suddenly, with the scalding fear that Miriam had been tugged out to sea while he remained, helpless and quite naked on the shore, their so-young bodies, only a moment before, exulting in everything that surrounded them: that was a horror which should not return and return. Is nothing ever ended?

Spirit Wrestlers

Thomas Shapcott

Spirit Wrestlers is a haunting, poetic novel by one of Australia's finest writers.

It tells of the arrival in rural Australia of a strange religious sect, an ancient Russian primitive group who believe in hard work, pacifism, vegetarianism – and the power of fire.

The group maintains a mysterious, closed existence that nevertheless begins to affect surrounding communities and individual lives. Two teenagers, Johann and Ivan, the local and the newcomer, discover similarities, and differences.

Spirit Wrestlers is a novel about faith, and competing faiths, acts of terror and acts of peace. In language of considerable beauty it speaks straight to the heart about our unsettled, dangerous world.

Follow Johann, Ivan and Olga in a saga of passion, surprise and discovery that you'll never forget.

Wakefield Press is an independent publishing and
distribution company based in Adelaide, South Australia.
We love good stories and publish beautiful books.
To see our full range of titles, please visit our website at
www.wakefieldpress.com.au.